If This New Megan Tried To Play On His Sympathy, It Wasn't Going To Work.

So help him, whatever it took, he was going to nail her to the wall.

She'd been looking straight ahead, but now she turned toward him with a frown. "Is something wrong, Cal? Another crisis back home?"

He managed a wry laugh. "Not that I know of. I could say I was just passing through and decided to stop by...." He saw the flash of skepticism in her caramel-colored eyes. "But you wouldn't believe me, would you?"

"No." A smile tugged a corner of her luscious mouth. The sort of mouth made for kissing. When was the last time she'd been kissed? he caught himself wondering.

But never mind that. He was here for just one reason.

Although, if getting to the truth involved kissing her, he wouldn't complain.

* * *

If you're on Twitter,
tell us what you think of Harlequin Desire!
#harlequindesire

Dear Reader,

Nothing seems small in Africa. It is a place of vast landscapes, spectacular animals, great beauty and unthinkable hardship. The people I met there were as poor as any on earth, yet their capacity for joy touched and inspired me.

After spending two weeks on safari in Tanzania, I knew I wanted to visit it again and take you, my readers, with me to share the experience. *A Sinful Seduction* is a story of loss and redemption, sacrifice, passion and danger all in a magnificent setting.

When Cal Jeffords's best friend and partner commits suicide, leaving millions in embezzled charity funds unaccounted for, Cal suspects Nick's glamorous widow, Megan, of the theft and vows to see her punished. But Megan has fled the country and is nowhere to be found. Two years later a hired detective tracks her down in Africa, serving as a volunteer nurse in the refugee camps of Sudan.

Surprised that she isn't living in luxury off the stolen money, Cal will do anything to get the truth from her. That includes taking her on a luxury safari and using his charm to seduce her. But Megan is wounded in body and spirit, and as they spend time together, Cal discovers that revenge and money are the least of his concerns.

I hope you enjoy this passionate adventure of the heart. I love hearing from my readers. You can contact me through my website, www.elizabethlaneauthor.com.

Happy reading,

Elizabeth

A SINFUL
SEDUCTION

—

ELIZABETH LANE

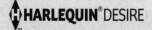

Recycling programs
for this product may
not exist in your area.

ISBN-13: 978-0-373-73323-1

A SINFUL SEDUCTION

Copyright © 2014 by Elizabeth Lane

All rights reserved. Except for use in any review, the reproduction
or utilization of this work in whole or in part in any form by any
electronic, mechanical or other means, now known or hereafter
invented, including xerography, photocopying and recording, or in
any information storage or retrieval system, is forbidden without
the written permission of the publisher, Harlequin Enterprises Limited,
225 Duncan Mill Road, Don Mills, Ontario M3B 3K9, Canada.

This is a work of fiction. Names, characters, places and incidents are
either the product of the author's imagination or are used fictitiously, and
any resemblance to actual persons, living or dead, business establishments,
events or locales is entirely coincidental.

This edition published by arrangement with Harlequin Books S.A.

For questions and comments about the quality of this book, please contact us
at CustomerService@Harlequin.com.

® and TM are trademarks of Harlequin Enterprises Limited or its corporate
affiliates. Trademarks indicated with ® are registered in the United States Patent
and Trademark Office, the Canadian Trade Marks Office and in other countries.

Printed in U.S.A.

www.Harlequin.com

Books by Elizabeth Lane

Harlequin Desire

In His Brother's Place #2208
The Santana Heir #2241
The Nanny's Secret #2277
A Sinful Seduction #2310

Harlequin Special Edition

Wild Wings, Wild Heart #936

Silhouette Romance

Hometown Wedding #1194
The Tycoon and the Townie #1250

Harlequin Historical

Wind River #28
Birds of Passage #92
Moonfire #150
MacKenna's Promise #216
Lydia #302
Apache Fire #436
Shawnee Bride #492
Bride on the Run #546
My Lord Savage #569
Navajo Sunrise #608
Christmas Gold #627
  "Jubal's Gift"
Wyoming Widow #657
Wyoming Wildcat #676
Wyoming Woman #728
Her Dearest Enemy #754
Wyoming Wildfire #792

Stay for Christmas #819
  "Angels in the Snow"
The Stranger #856
On The Wings of Love #881
The Borrowed Bride #920
His Substitute Bride #939
Cowboy Christmas #963
  "The Homecoming"
The Horseman's Bride #983
The Widowed Bride #1031
The Lawman's Vow #1079
Weddings Under a Western Sky #1091
  "The Hand-Me-Down Bride"
The Ballad of Emma O'Toole #1151

ELIZABETH LANE

has lived and traveled in many parts of the world, including Europe, Latin America and the Far East, but her heart remains in the American West, where she was born and raised. Her idea of heaven is hiking a mountain trail on a clear autumn day. She also enjoys music, animals and dancing. You can learn more about Elizabeth by visiting her website, www.elizabethlaneauthor.com.

For Pat, my wonderful sister who loves Africa

One

San Francisco, California, February 11

The headline on Page 2 slammed Cal Jeffords in the face.

Two Years Later
Exec's Widow, Foundation Cash
Are Both Still Missing

Swearing like a longshoreman, Cal crumpled the morning paper in his fist. The last thing he needed was a reminder that today was the second anniversary of his best friend and business partner's suicide. And he didn't need that grainy file photo to help him remember Nick and his wife, Megan, with her movie-star beauty, her designer clothes, her multimillion-dollar showplace of a home and her appalling lack of human decency that let her steal from a charity and then leave her husband to carry the blame.

With a grunt of frustration, he crammed the newspaper into the waste basket.

He had no doubt that the whole ugly mess was Megan's fault. But the questions that still haunted him two years later were *how* and *why?* Had Megan coerced Nick into complying? Had the demands of their lavish lifestyle driven Nick Rafferty to embezzle millions from J-COR's charity foundation? Or had Megan embezzled the money herself and forced her husband to take the blame? She'd had plenty of opportunities to siphon off the cash her fund-raisers brought in. He'd even found evidence that she had.

But Cal would never know for sure. The day after the scandal went public, he'd found Nick slumped over his desk, his hand still clutching the pistol that had ended his life. After the private funeral, Megan had vanished. The stolen money, meant to ease the suffering of third-world refugees, was never recovered.

It didn't take a genius to make the connection.

Too restless to sit, Cal unfolded his athletic frame and prowled to the window that spanned the outer wall. His office, on the twenty-eighth floor of the J-COR building, commanded a sweeping view of the Bay and the bridge that spanned the choppy, gray water. Beyond the Golden Gate, the stormy Pacific stretched as far as the eye could see.

Megan was out there somewhere. Cal could feel it, like a sickness in his bones. He could picture her in some far-away land, living like a maharani on the millions stolen from his foundation.

It wasn't so much the missing cash itself that troubled him—although the loss had cut into the foundation's resources. It was the sheer crassness of taking money earmarked for food, clean water and medical treatment in places rife with human misery. That Megan hadn't seen fit to make amends at any point after her husband's death made the crime even more despicable.

She could have returned the money, no questions asked. Even if she was innocent, as she'd claimed to be, she could have stayed around to help him locate it. Instead, she'd simply run, further cementing Cal's certainty of her guilt. She wouldn't have run if she didn't have something to hide. And the woman was damned good at hiding her trail. Not one of the investigators he'd hired had been able to track her down.

But Cal wasn't a man to give up. Someday he would find her. And when he did, one way or another, Megan Rafferty would pay.

"Mr. Jeffords."

Cal turned at the sound of his name. His receptionist stood in the office doorway. "Harlan Crandall's outside, asking to see you. Do you have time for him now, or should I schedule an appointment?"

"Send him in." Crandall was the latest in the string of private investigators Cal had hired to search for Megan. A short, balding man with an unassuming manner, he'd shown no more promise than the others. But now he'd come by unannounced, asking for an audience. Maybe he had something to report.

Cal seated himself as Crandall entered, wearing a rumpled brown suit and clutching a battered canvas briefcase.

"Sit down, Mr. Crandall." Cal motioned to the chair on the far side of the desk. "Do you have any news for me?"

"That depends." Crandall plopped the briefcase onto the desk, opened the flap and drew out a manila folder. "You hired me to look for Mrs. Rafferty. Do you happen to know her maiden name?"

"Of course, and so should you. It's Cardston. Megan Cardston."

Crandall nodded, adjusting his wire-rimmed glasses on his nose. "In that case, I may have something to tell you. My sources have tracked down a Megan Cardston who appears to fit the physical description of the woman you're looking for. She's working as a volunteer nurse for your foundation."

Cal's reflexes jerked. "That's impossible," he growled. "It's got to be a coincidence—just another woman with the same name and body type."

"Maybe so. You can decide for yourself after you've looked over this documentation." Crandall thrust the folder across the desk.

Cal opened the folder. It contained several photocopied pages that looked like travel requests and personnel rosters. But what caught his eye was a single, blurry black-and-white photograph.

Staring at the image, he tried to picture Megan as he'd last seen her—long platinum hair sculpted into a twist, diamond earrings, flawless makeup. Even at her husband's funeral, she'd managed to look like a Hollywood screen goddess, except for her pain-shot eyes.

The woman in the photo appeared thinner and slightly older. She was wearing sunglasses and a khaki shirt. Her light brown hair was short and windblown, her face bare of makeup. There was nothing behind her but sky.

Cal studied the firm jawline, the aristocratic nose and ripe, sensual lips. He willed himself to ignore the quiver of certainty that passed through his body. Megan's face was seared into his memory. Even with her eyes hidden, the woman in the picture had the same look. And Megan, he recalled, had worked as a surgical nurse before marrying Nick. But was this image really the woman who'd eluded him for two long years? There was only one way to be sure.

"Where was this picture taken?" he demanded. "Where's this woman now?"

Crandall slid the briefcase off the desk and closed it with a snap and a single word.

"Africa."

Arusha, Tanzania, February 26

Megan gripped the birth-slicked infant and delivered a stinging fingertip blow to its tiny buttocks.

Nothing happened.

She slapped the baby harder, her lips moving in a wordless plea. There was a beat of silence, then, suddenly, a gasping wail, as beautiful as any sound she'd ever heard. Megan's knees slackened in relief. The delivery had been hellish, a breech birth coming after a long night of labor. That mother and baby were both alive could only be counted as a miracle.

Passing the baby to the young aide, she mopped her brow with the sleeve of her smock, then reached over to do the same for the baby's mother. The air was warm and sticky. Light from a single bulb flickered on whitewashed walls. Drawn by the glow, insects beat against the screened windows.

As Megan leaned over her, the woman's eyelids fluttered open. *"Asante sana,"* she whispered in Swahili, the lingua franca of East Africa. *Thank you.*

"Karibu sana." Megan's deft hands wound a cotton string, knotted it tight and severed the cord. With luck, this baby would grow up healthy, spared the swollen belly and scarecrow limbs of the children she'd labored so desperately to save in Darfur, the most brutally ravaged region of Sudan, where a cruel dictator had used his mercenaries to decimate the African tribal population.

Megan had spent the past eleven months working with the J-COR Foundation's medical branch in the Sudanese refugee camps. Two weeks ago, on the brink of physical and emotional collapse, she'd been ordered to a less taxing post for recovery. Compared with the camps, this clinic, on the ramshackle fringe of a pleasant Tanzanian town, was a luxury resort.

But she would go back as soon as she was strong enough. She'd spent too many years feeling purposeless and adrift. Now that she'd found focus in her life, she was determined to finally make the most of her skills and training. She should be where she was needed most. And she was sorely needed in Darfur.

By the time the afterbirth came, the aide had sponged the baby boy clean and swaddled him in cotton flannel. The mother's eager hands reached out to draw him against her breast. Megan took a moment to raise the sheet and check the gauze packing. So far, everything looked all right. She stripped off her smock and her latex gloves. "I'm going to get some rest," she told the aide. "Watch her. Too much blood, you come and wake me."

The young African nurse-in-training nodded. She could be counted on to do her job.

Not until she was soaping her hands at the outside faucet did Megan realize how weary she was. It was as if the last of her strength had trickled down her legs and drained into the hard-packed earth. Straightening, she massaged her lower back with her fingers.

Beyond the clinic's corrugated roof, the moon glimmered like a lost shilling through the purple crown of a flowering jacaranda. Its low angle told her the time was well past midnight, with precious few hours left for sleep. All too soon, first light would trigger a cacophony of bird calls, signaling the start of a new day. At least she'd ended the day well—with a successful delivery and a healthy new life. The sense of accomplishment was strong.

Tired as she was, Megan knew she had no right to complain. This was the life she'd chosen. By now her old life—the clothes and jewelry, the cars, the house, the charity events she'd hosted to raise money for Nick and Cal's foundation—seemed little more than a dream. A dream that had ended with a headline and a gunshot.

She'd tried not to dwell on that nightmare week. But one image was chiseled into her memory—Cal's stricken face, the look of cold contempt in his glacial gray eyes, and the final words he'd spoken to her.

"You're going to answer for this, Megan. I'll hold you accountable and make you pay if it's the last thing I do."

Megan hadn't embezzled a cent, hadn't even known about the missing money till the scandal had surfaced. But Cal would never believe that. He'd trusted Nick to the very last.

Seeing Cal's look and hearing his words, Megan had realized she had no recourse except to run far and fast, to someplace where Cal would never find her.

That, or be trapped with no way to save her own soul.

But all that was in the past, she reminded herself as she flexed her aching shoulders and mounted the porch of the brick bungalow that served as quarters for the volunteers. She was a different person now, with a life that gave her the deepest satisfaction she had ever known.

If only she could put an end to the nightmares….

As the sleek Gulfstream jet skimmed the Horn of Africa, Cal reopened the folder Harlan Crandall had given him. Clever fellow, that Crandall. He alone had thought to look in the last place Megan would logically choose to hide—the volunteer ranks of the very foundation she had robbed.

The photocopied paperwork gave him a summary of her postings—Zimbabwe, Somalia and, for most of the past year, Sudan. Megan had taken the roughest assignments in the program—evidently by her own choice. What was she thinking? And if the woman in the photo was really Nick's glamorous widow, what in hell's name had she done with the money? She'd stolen enough to live in luxury for decades. Luxury even more ostentatious than the lifestyle her husband had given her.

Cal couldn't repress a sigh as he thought of the expensive trappings Nick had lavished on his wife. He'd always wanted her to have nothing but the best. His taste might have been over-the-top, but Cal had always been certain that Nick's intentions were good, just as they had been back when the two had become friends in high school.

They'd graduated from the same college, Cal with an engineering degree and Nick with a marketing major. When Cal had come up with a design for a lightweight modular shelter that could be erected swiftly in the wake of a natural disaster or used at construction and recreation sites, it had made sense for the two friends to go into business together. J-COR had made them both wealthy. But they'd agreed that money wasn't enough. After providing shelters for stricken people around the world, it had been Cal's idea to set up a foundation. He'd handled the logistics end. Nick had managed the finances and fund-raising.

Within a few years the foundation had expanded to include food and medical services. By then Nick was married to Megan, a nurse he'd met at a fund-raiser. Cal had been best man at their wedding. But even then he hadn't quite trusted her. She was too beautiful. Too gracious.

Too private. Beneath that polished surface he'd glimpsed something elusive; something hidden.

Her cool distance was a striking contrast to Nick's natural openness and warmth—particularly given the way Nick clearly doted on her. He had showered his bride with gifts—a multimillion-dollar house, a Ferrari, a diamond-and-emerald necklace and more. Megan had responded by using her new position in society to supposedly "help" the foundation. The charity events they'd hosted for wealthy donors at their home had raised generous amounts for the foundation. But of course, those events had done much more to line Megan's pockets. Three years later, after a routine tax audit, the whole house of cards had come tumbling down. The rest of the story was tabloid fodder.

Cal studied the photograph, which looked as if it had been snapped at a distance and enlarged for his benefit. Megan—if that's who it really was—may not have even known it was being taken. She was gazing to her left, the light glinting on her sunglasses—expensive sunglasses. Cal noticed the side logo for the first time. He remembered her wearing that brand, maybe that very pair. His mouth tightened as the certainty slid into place. Megan hadn't quite abandoned her high-end tastes.

It was a piece of luck that she'd been sent to Arusha. Finding her in Sudan could have involved a grueling search. But Arusha, a bustling tourist and safari center, had its own international airport. The company jet was headed there now, and he knew how to find the clinic. He'd been there before. If he so chose, he could round her up with the help of some hired muscle and have her on the plane within a couple of hours.

And then what? Tempting as the idea was, Cal knew it wasn't practical to kidnap her in a foreign country without a legal warrant. Besides, would it do any good if he could?

Megan was smart. She'd know that despite her signature on the checks that had never made it to the foundation's coffers, he had no solid proof she'd kept the money. If she stuck to her original story, that she'd had no knowledge of the theft and knew nothing about the missing funds, he'd be nowhere.

He didn't have grounds or authority to arrest her; and it wasn't in him to threaten her with physical harm. His only hope of getting at the truth, Cal realized, was to win her trust. He wasn't optimistic enough to think he could make her confess. She was too smart to openly admit to her crimes. But if he got close to her, she might let something slip—drop a tiny clue, innocent on its own, that could lead Crandall to the location of the hidden accounts.

That could take time. But he hadn't come this far to go home without answers. If that meant wining and dining the lady and telling her a few pretty lies, so be it.

The slight dip in the angle of the cabin told him the plane was starting its descent. If the weather was clear, he might get a look at the massive cone of Kilimanjaro. But that was not to be. Clouds were gathering off the right wing, hiding the view of the fabled mountain. Lightning chained across the distant sky. The seasonal rains had begun. If this kept up, which it likely would, they'd be landing in an African downpour.

Fastening his seat belt, Cal settled back to watch the storm approach. The plane shuddered as lightning snaked over its metal skin. Rain spattered the windows, the sound of it recalling another time, a rainy night three years ago in San Francisco.

It had been the night of the company Christmas party, held downtown at the Hilton. At about eleven o'clock Cal had bumped into Megan coming out of the hallway that led to the restrooms. Her face was white, her mouth damp, as if she'd just splashed it with water. Cal had stopped to ask if she was all right.

She'd laughed. "I'm fine, Cal. Just a little bit…pregnant."

"Can I get you anything?" he'd asked, surprised that Nick hadn't told him.

"No, thanks. Since Nick has to stay, I'm going to have him call me a cab. No more late-night parties for this girl."

She'd hurried away, leaving Cal to reflect that in all the time he'd known her, this was the first time he'd seen Megan look truly happy.

Was she happy now? He tried to picture her working in a refugee camp—the heat, the flies, the poverty, the sickness…. What was she doing here? What had she done with the money? The questions tormented him—and only one person could give him the answers.

Megan sank onto a bench outside the clinic, sheltered from the rain by the overhanging roof. The day had been hectic, as usual. The new mother and her baby were gone, carted off by her womenfolk early that morning. Her departure had been followed by a flood of patients with ailments ranging from impetigo to malaria. Megan had even assisted while the resident Tanzanian doctor stitched up and vaccinated a boy who'd been foolish enough to tease a young baboon.

Now it was twilight and the clinic was closed. The doctor and the aide had gone home to their families in town. Megan was alone in the walled compound that included the clinic building, a generator and washhouse, a lavatory and a two-room bungalow with a kitchen for volunteers like her. The utilitarian brick structures were softened by the flowering shrubs and trees that flourished in Arusha's rich volcanic soil. The tulip tree that shaded the clinic had ended its blooming cycle. Rain washed the fallen petals in a crimson cascade off the eave, like tears of blood.

Closing her eyes, Megan inhaled the sweet dampness. She'd yearned for rain in the parched Sudan, where the dusty air was rank with the odors of human misery. Going back wouldn't be easy. But the need was too great for her not to return. The need of the refugees for care and treatment—and her own need to make a difference.

She was about to get up and brave the downpour when she heard the clang of the gate bell—an improvised iron cowbell on a chain. Rising, she hesitated. If someone had an emergency she could hardly turn them away. But she was here alone. Outside that gate there could be thugs intent on breaking into the clinic for drugs, cash or mischief.

The bell jangled again. Megan sprinted through the rain to the bungalow, found the .38 Smith & Wesson she kept under her pillow and thrust it into the pocket of her loose khakis. Grabbing a plastic poncho from its hook by the door, she tossed it over her head as she hurried toward the sheet-iron gate. The key was in the rusty padlock that anchored the chain between the gate's welded handles.

"Jina lako nani?" she demanded in her phrase-book Swahili. She'd asked for the person's name, which was the best she could manage.

There was a beat of silence. Then a gravely, masculine voice rang through the rainy darkness. "Megan? Is that you?"

Megan's knees crumpled like wet sand. She sagged against the gate, her cold hands fumbling with the key. Cal's was the last voice she wanted to hear. But hiding from him would only make her look like a fool.

"Megan?" His voice had taken on a more strident tone, demanding an answer. But her throat was too tight to speak. She should have known that Cal wouldn't give up looking until he found her—even if he had to travel half-way around the world.

The lock fell open, allowing the heavy chain to slide free. Megan stepped back as the gate swung inward and Cal strode into the courtyard. Dressed in a tan Burberry raincoat, he seemed even taller than she remembered, his gray eyes even colder behind the rain that dripped off the brim of his hat.

She knew what he wanted. After two years, Cal was still looking for answers. Now that he'd found her, he would hammer her mercilessly with questions about Nick's death and the whereabouts of the stolen money.

But she had no answers to give him.

How could she persuade Cal Jeffords to see the truth and leave her in peace?

Two

Cal's eyes took in the cheap plastic poncho and the tired face beneath the hood. Something in his chest jerked tight. It was Megan, all right. But not the Megan he remembered.

"Hello, Cal." Her voice was rich and husky. "I see you haven't changed much."

"But you have." He turned and fastened the gate behind him. "Aren't you at least going to invite me out of the rain?"

She glanced toward the bungalow. "I can make you some coffee. But there's not much else. I haven't had time to shop…" Her voice trailed off as she led him through the downpour to the sheltered porch. Rain clattered on the corrugated tin roof above their heads.

"Actually I have a taxi waiting outside," he said. "I was hoping I could take you to dinner at the hotel."

Her eyes widened. She seemed nervous, he thought.

But then, she had plenty to hide. "That's kind of you, but there's no one else here. I need to stay—"

He laid a hand on her shoulder. She quivered like a fawn at his touch but didn't try to pull away. "It's all right," he said. "I spoke with Dr. Musa on the phone. It's fine with him if you leave for a couple of hours. In fact, he said you could use a nice meal. His houseboy's on the way over now, to watch the place while we're gone."

"Well, since it's all arranged…" Her voice trailed off.

"Dr. Musa also mentioned that you're doing a great job here." That part was true, but Cal made a point of saying it to flatter her.

She shrugged, a slight motion. The old Megan would have lapped up the praise like a satisfied cat. This thin-drawn stranger seemed uncomfortable with it. "I've just finished cleaning up in the clinic. I'll need to wash and change." She managed a strained laugh. "These days it doesn't take long."

"Fine. I'll open the gate for the cab."

As Cal slogged back across the compound, he spared a moment to be grateful that he'd thought to bring a pair of waterproof hiking boots before his thoughts returned to his encounter with the woman he'd come to find. Meeting Megan tonight was like meeting her for the first time. He was puzzled and intrigued, but still determined to get to the bottom of the money question. If this new Megan tried to play on his sympathy—and she likely would—it wasn't going to work. So help him, whatever it took, he was going to nail her to the wall.

Minutes after the cab pulled up to the bungalow, Benjamin, Dr. Musa's strapping young servant, arrived. Megan emerged from her room wearing a white blouse, fresh khaki slacks and a black twill jacket. A corner of the folded plastic poncho stuck out of her beat-up brown leather purse—Gucci, he noticed the brand. Some things at least hadn't changed.

Giving Benjamin her pistol, she thanked him with a smile and a few words. Cal lifted a side of his raincoat like a wing to shelter her as they descended the porch steps and climbed into the cab. Her face was damp, her hair finger-combed. She hadn't taken more than ten minutes to freshen up and change, but it had worked. She looked damned classy.

"When did you get in?" she asked him, making small talk.

"Plane landed a couple of hours ago. I registered at the Arusha Hotel, cleaned up and headed for the clinic."

She'd been looking straight ahead, but now she turned toward him with a frown. "Is something wrong, Cal? A crisis back home?"

He managed a wry laugh. "Not that I know of. I could say I was just passing through and decided to stop by..." He saw the flash of skepticism in her caramel-colored eyes. "But you wouldn't believe me, would you?"

"No." A smile tugged a corner of her luscious mouth. The sort of mouth made for kissing. Though he had never warmed to her personally, he'd never denied that she was an attractive and desirable woman. When was the last time she'd been kissed? he caught himself wondering. But never mind that. He was here for just one reason. Although, if getting to the truth involved kissing her, he wouldn't complain.

"I know you better than that, Cal. I left you with a lot of questions. But if you're here to charm the answers out of me, you could've saved yourself a trip. Nothing's changed. I don't know anything about where you could find the money. I'm assuming Nick spent it—which, I suppose, makes me guilty by association. But if you're looking for a big stash under my mattress or in some Dubai bank account, all I can do is wish you luck."

It was like her to be direct, Cal thought. That trait, at least, hadn't changed. "Why don't we table that subject for now. I'm more interested in why you left and what you've been doing for the past two years."

"Of course you are." Something glimmered in her eyes before she glanced away. The cab's windshield wipers swished and thumped in the stillness. Rain streamed down the windows. "For the price of a good steak, I suppose I can come up with a few good stories—entertaining, if nothing else."

"You never disappoint." Cal kept his voice as neutral as his comment. He had yet to pin down this new Megan. The inner steel she'd always possessed gleamed below a surface so fragile that he sensed she might shatter at a touch.

He knew she'd been sent here for rest and recovery. Nothing in the documents he'd seen explained why, but Dr. Musa, the tall, British-trained Chagga who ran the clinic, had expressed his concern about her health and state of mind to Cal over the phone. Cal needed to learn more. But right now, he was still taking in her presence.

He recalled the perfume she used to wear. The fancy French name of it eluded him, but he'd always found it mildly arousing. There was no trace of that scent now. If she smelled like anything at all, it was the medicinal soap used in the clinic. But strangely, her nearness in the cab was having the same effect on him as that perfume used to have back then.

Things were different now. Back in San Francisco she'd been his best friend's wife. Megan had been widowed for two years, and if there was anyone else in her life, there was no mention of it in Crandall's report. As long as the end justified the means, bedding her would be a long-

denied pleasure. A little pillow talk could go a long way
in loosening secrets.

If nothing else, it would be damned delicious fun.

Megan had spent little time outside the clinic since her
arrival, so the remodeled nineteenth-century Arusha Hotel
was new to her. Catering to wealthy tourists, it featured
a lobby decorated in rich creams and browns with wing-
back chairs and dark leather sofas, a bar and a restaurant
with an international menu. Through the glass doors at the
rear of the lobby, she glimpsed a large outdoor swimming
pool, deserted tonight except for the rain that whipped the
water to a froth.

Cal's big hand rested beneath her elbow as he ushered
her toward the restaurant. Megan was of average height,
but she felt small next to him. He was almost six-three,
broad-shouldered and athletic, with a hard-charging manner that defied anyone to stand in his way. John Wayne in
an Armani suit—that was how she would have described
him back in the day. Even tonight, in travel-creased khakis,
he looked imposing. John Wayne in the old movie *Hatari*
came to mind—maybe because it was also the name of
the hotel bar. She'd always found Nick's best friend over-
bearing. But there'd been times when she'd wished her
husband was more like him.

She wasn't surprised that he'd found her. Once he set
his mind, Cal Jeffords could be as fiercely determined as
a pit bull. And he'd come too far to leave without getting
something to make his trip worthwhile. She'd told him the
truth about the money. But he hadn't even pretended
to believe her. Her signature on the donation checks she'd
endorsed and given to Nick to deposit had convinced him
she was guilty. Megan's instincts told her he had a plan to
wear her down and make her pay. It would do her no good

to fight. Cal was as much a force of nature as the storm raging outside. All she could do was wait for it to pass.

Sitting at their quiet table, she allowed him to order for her—filet mignon with mushrooms, fresh organic vegetables and a vintage Merlot. She could feel his gaze on her as the white-gloved waiter filled their wine goblets and set a basket of fresh hot bread between the lighted candlesticks.

"Eat up," Cal said, raising his glass. "You need to put some meat on those lovely bones."

Megan broke off a corner of the bread and nibbled at the crust. "I know I've lost weight. But it's painful to fill your plate when people around you are starving."

His slate gray eyes narrowed. "Is that what this is all about—this life change of yours? Guilt?"

She shrugged. "When I was married to Nick, I thought I had it all—the big house, the cars, the parties…" She took a sip of the wine. The sweet tingle burned down her throat. "When it all fell apart, and I learned that my lifestyle was literally taking food out of people's mouths, it sickened me. So, yes, you can call it guilt. Call it whatever you want. Does it matter? I don't regret the choice I made."

A muscle twitched in his cheek, betraying a surge of tightly reined anger. "The choice to run away without telling me? Without telling anybody?"

"Yes." She met his eyes with her own level gaze. "Nick left a god-awful mess behind. If I hadn't run, I'd still be back in San Francisco trying to clean it up."

"I know. I had to clean up most of it myself."

"There wasn't much I could do to help. The house was mortgaged to the rafters—something I didn't know until the bank called me after Nick's death. I told them to go ahead and take it. And the cars were in Nick's name, not mine. I'm assuming your company took those, along with the art and the furniture. I boxed up my clothes and shoes

for Goodwill and pawned my jewelry for travel money—
cash only. I knew my credit cards could be traced."

"By me?"

"Yes. But also by the reporters who kept hounding me
and the police who seemed to think I'd have a different
answer the fiftieth time they asked a question than I did
the first."

"If you'd stayed, I could have made things easier for
both of us, Megan."

"How could I take that chance? I knew the questions
from the police, from the press and from you wouldn't
stop. But, so help me, Cal, I didn't have any answers. It
was easier to just vanish. I was half hoping you'd believe
I'd died. In a way, I had."

The waiter had reappeared with their dinners. Megan
half expected Cal to start grilling her about the missing
funds, but he only glanced toward her plate in an unspoken order to eat her meal.

The steak was surprisingly tender, but Megan's anxiety
had robbed her of appetite. She took small bites, glancing across the table like a mouse nibbling the cheese in
a baited trap. Her eyes studied Cal's craggy face, trying
to catch some nuance of expression. Was he about to trip
the spring?

He'd aged subtly in the past two years. The shadows had
darkened around his deep-set eyes, and his sandy hair was
lightly brushed with gray. Nick's betrayal and suicide had
wounded him, too, she realized. Like her, Cal was dealing
with the pain in his own way.

"I was just wondering," he said. "When you joined that
first project in Zimbabwe, was the director aware of who
you were?"

"No. He was a local, and Zimbabwe's a long way from
San Francisco. My passport was still in my maiden name,

so that was the name I used. I showed up, described my nursing training and offered my help at the AIDS clinic. They needed a nurse too badly to ask many questions."

"And the transfers?"

"Once I got on the permanent volunteer roster, I could go pretty much where I wanted. Early on I was nervous about staying in one place too long. I moved around a lot. After a while it didn't seem to matter."

"And in Darfur? What happened there?"

The question shook her. Something too vague to be called a memory twisted inside, silent and cold like the coils of a snake. Megan willed herself not to feel it.

"You were there for eleven months," he persisted. "They sent you here for recovery. Something must have gotten to you."

She shrugged, her unease growing as she stared down at the weave of the bright brown-and-yellow tablecloth. "It's nothing. I just need rest, that's all. I'll be ready to go back in a couple of weeks."

"That's not what Dr. Musa told me. He says you have panic attacks. And you won't talk about what happened."

Megan's anxiety exploded in outrage. "He had no right to tell you that. And you had no right to ask him."

"My foundation's paying his salary. That gives me the right." Cal's leaden gray eyes drilled her like bullets. "Dr. Musa thinks you have post-traumatic stress. Whatever happened out there, Megan, you're not going back until you deal with it. So you might as well tell me now."

He was pushing too hard, backing her against an invisible wall. The dark coils twisted and tightened inside her. Sensing what was about to happen, she willed herself to lay down her fork. It clattered onto her plate. "I don't remember, all right?" Her voice emerged thin and raw. "It doesn't matter. I just need some time to myself and I'll be

fine. And now, if you don't mind, I need to get back to…
the clinic."

Her voice broke on the last words. As her self-control
began to crumble, she rose, flung her linen napkin onto
the table, caught up her purse and walked swiftly out of the
restaurant. There had to be a ladies' room close by, where
she could shut herself in a stall and huddle until her heart
stopped thundering. Experience had taught her to recog-
nize the symptoms of a panic attack. But short of doping
herself with tranquilizers, she had little control over the
rush of irrational terror that flooded her body.

She reached the lobby and glanced around for the rest-
room sign. The desk clerk was busy. No matter, she could
find it by herself. But where was it? She could hear her
heart, pounding in her ears.

Where was it?

Caught off guard, Cal stared after her for an instant.
Then he shoved out his chair, stood and strode after her.
She hadn't made it far. He found her in the lobby, her
wide-eyed gaze darting this way and that like a cornered
animal's.

Without a word, he caught her shoulders, forcing her to
turn inward against his chest. She resisted, but feebly, her
body shaking. "Leave me alone," she muttered. "I'm fine."

"You're not fine. Come on." He guided her forcefully
through the lobby and out the back door to the patio. Sheltered by the overhanging roof, they stood veiled by a curtain of rain. Her body was rigid in his arms. He could feel
her heart pounding against his chest, feel the slight pressure of her breasts. She'd stopped fighting him, but the
trembling continued. Her breath came in muted gasps.
Her fists balled the fabric of his shirt.

He might not be the most sensitive guy in the world, but even he could tell that the woman was terrified.

What had she been through? Cal had visited the Sudan refugee camps—a hell of human misery if ever there was one. Tens of thousands of people crammed into tents and makeshift shelters, not enough food, not enough water, open sewers and latrines teeming with disease. Organizations like the United Nations and private, nongovernment charities, known as NGOs, did what they could. But the need was overwhelming. And Megan had spent eleven months there.

He wouldn't have been surprised to find her dispirited and worn down—which she clearly was. But there was something more here. Harsh conditions wouldn't have made her this fearful. Something had happened specifically to her. Something so terrifying that the briefest reminder of it was enough to make her quake.

He was here about the money, he reminded himself. She was guilty as hell, and he couldn't let himself be moved by sympathy. But right now Megan's need for comfort appeared all too real. And besides, hadn't he wanted to get close to her—close enough to learn her secrets? Here was his chance to take that first step.

"It's all right, girl," he muttered against her silky hair. "You're safe here. I've got you."

His hand massaged her back beneath the light jacket. She was bone thin, the back of her bra stretched tight across shoulder blades that jutted like wings. He'd come here to get the truth out of her and see that she was punished for any part she might have played in Nick's suicide. But arriving at that truth would take time and patience. Megan was fragile in body and wounded in spirit. Pushing her too hard could shatter what few reserves she had left.

Not that Cal was a saint. Far from it, as his hardening

arousal bore witness. It might have been an indelicate response to the situation, but it was the only way he knew to reply. His relationships were usually short-lived affairs, with plenty of heat that burned out quickly. With all the time he devoted to J-COR and the foundation, he had little to spare for romantic entanglements. Brief, passionate flings were usually his preference—the sort of relationship shallow enough for every conflict to be solved by taking matters to bed. He had little experience comforting genuine distress, and his body shifted into default mode, wanting to solve the problem by replacing her troubled thoughts—and his own niggling guilt for causing her such distress—with ecstasy for them both.

The desire was there, smoldering where her hips rested against his, igniting the urge to sweep her upstairs to his luxury suite and ravish her till she moaned with pleasure. Maybe that was what the woman needed—a few weeks of rest, good food and good loving to restore her health and build her trust.

But that wasn't going to happen tonight. It was comfort and support she needed now, not some big, horny jerk making moves on her.

Giving himself a mental slap, Cal shifted backward, easing the contact between them. She was calm now. Maybe too calm. "Want to talk about it?" he asked.

She exhaled, pushing away from him. "I'll be fine. Sorry you had to see me like that. I feel like a fool."

"No one's blaming you. I've seen those camps. You've been through eleven months of hell."

"But not like the people who have nowhere else to go. Seeing their children die, their women—"

"You can't dwell on that, Megan."

"I can't forget it. That's why I plan to go back as soon as I'm strong enough."

"That's insane. I could stop you, you know."

"You could try. But if you do, I'll find another way."

The defiance in her gaze stunned him. Back in San Francisco, where he'd known her as a charming hostess and a lovely ornament, he would never have believed she could possess such an iron will. But her will looked to be all she had left. She was like a guttering candle, on the verge of burning out.

"You should go back and finish your dinner," she said. "I've got my rain poncho. I can catch a *matatu* back to the clinic."

"One of those rickety little buses? You'd end up walking for blocks, alone in the rain. I'll take you." Cal wouldn't have minded inviting her upstairs for a hot bath and a chaste, restful night in his suite's second bed—as a simple act of kindness. But she was certain to turn him down. And even if she accepted, he didn't trust himself to behave. For all her devious ways, Megan was an alluring woman, made more so by her surprising strength and the unspoken challenge in her manner. The urge to bury himself between those slim, lovely legs might prove too much to resist.

But an idea had taken root in his thoughts—one so audacious that it surprised even him. First thing tomorrow he would make some calls. What he had in mind might be just the thing to restore her health and win her trust.

Minutes later Megan was huddled beside Cal in the cab's backseat. The rain had stopped, but the night was chilly and the black blazer she'd worn to look presentable was too thin for warmth.

"You're shivering." Cal peeled off his Burberry coat and wrapped it around her shoulders, enfolding her in the heat and manly scent of his body. A thread of panic uncurled inside her. She willed it away.

"We've talked about me all evening," she said, making conversation. "What's new with you?"

"Nothing much, except that I'm here. The company's doing fine. So is the foundation. I've hired a team of professionals to do the fund-raising. But they don't have your elegant touch. I miss you and...Nick."

Megan hadn't missed the beat of hesitation before he spoke her late husband's name. "That time seems like a hundred years ago," she said, then tactfully changed the subject. "Any special lady in your life? As I recall, you always had plenty to choose from."

"Having a special lady requires an investment in time. More time than I can spare."

"Remind yourself of that when you're a grumpy, lonely old man," she teased. "You're what? Forty?"

"Thirty-eight. Don't make me out to be more decrepit than I already am."

"Fine. But one of these days you're going to look back and wish you'd had a family."

"You're a fine one to talk," he countered.

"Well, at least I tried." She remembered telling him about the baby. Had Nick let him know she'd miscarried? Or had her statement made him think of her wedding day, when his best man's toast had congratulated the two of them on the new family they were making together?

His answering silence told Megan she'd pushed the conversation onto painful ground. Cal had been as devastated as she was by Nick's death. Devastated and angry—or at least, there had been anger on *her* part, when she'd learned about the embezzlement. Cal had seemed determined to find some way to clear Nick of any blame...which had meant shoving that blame on her, instead. Now, more than two years and half a world away, she was sitting beside him with his coat wrapped around her. It was as if they'd come full circle. She'd done everything in her power to put the past behind her and find peace. But it was no use. Being with Cal had brought it all back.

Three

Cal had offered Benjamin a cab ride back to Dr. Musa's. The distance wasn't far but by the time they arrived, jet lag from the long flight had caught up with him. He was nodding off every few minutes.

"Won't you come in, sir?" the husky youth asked as he climbed out of the cab. "I can make you tea."

"Another time, thank you. And give my best to the doctor. Tell him I'll ring him up tomorrow."

As the cab headed on to the hotel, splashing through the backstreet ruts, Cal reflected on his evening with Megan. Nothing had been as he'd expected. She was so fragile, and yet so powerfully seductive that he'd been caught off guard. It would have been all too easy to forget that the woman had either stolen or driven his best friend to steal millions from the foundation before killing himself, and that the money was still missing. In the days ahead he'd do well to remember that.

A few evenings out weren't going to break down her resistance. He was going to need more time with her—a lot more time, in a setting calculated to put her at ease. A safari would be perfect—days exploring Africa's beautiful wildlands, and the kind of pampered nights that a first-class safari company could provide.

Tomorrow he would put his scheme into action. First, as a courtesy, he would ask Dr. Musa's permission to take Megan out of the clinic for a couple of weeks. If need be, he could fly in another volunteer to take her place. Arranging a photo safari on short notice shouldn't be a problem. Business tended to slow during the rainy season. Most companies would be eager to accommodate a well-paying client.

Not until everything was in place would he let Megan in on his plan. She might argue. She might even dig in her heels and refuse to go along. But in the end she would go with him. If he had to knock her out and kidnap her, so help him, she would go.

Evenings were long and peaceful on safari, with little to do except eat, drink, rest and talk. As for the nights… But he would let nature take its course. If things went as planned, Megan would soon be stripped of any secrets she was hiding.

But first he wanted to cover all his bases. Tomorrow he would compose an email to Harlan Crandall. If the man was sharp enough to locate Megan, he might also be able to ferret out more details about the last months of Nick's life. He might even be able to locate the missing money.

For now—Cal punctuated the thought with a tired yawn—all he wanted was to go back to the hotel, crawl between the sheets and sleep off his jet lag.

On a cot veiled by mosquito netting, Megan writhed in fitful sleep. Her hellish dreams varied from night to night.

But this one from her time in Darfur dominated them all, replaying as if it had been burned into her brain.

Saida had been just fifteen, a beautiful child with liquid brown eyes and the doelike grace of her people, the Fur. Because she spoke fair English, and because her family was dead, Megan had given her a translating job at the camp infirmary, with an out-of-the-way corner for sleeping. Bright with promise, Saida had one failing. She had fallen in love with a boy named Gamal, and love had made her careless. Checking on the patients late one night, Megan had found Saida's pallet empty. Earlier, the starry-eyed girl had mentioned her trysting place with Gamal, a dry well outside the camp. That had to be where she'd gone.

Leaving the camp at night was forbidden. Beyond the boundaries, bands of rogue Janjaweed mercenaries prowled the desert like wild dogs in search of prey. No one was safe out there. Megan had known that she needed to find the two foolish youngsters and bring them back before the unthinkable happened. Arming herself with a loaded pistol, she'd plunged into the darkness.

Now the dream swirled around her like an evil mist. She was sprinting through pools of shadow, the waning moon a razor edge of light above the naked hills. Behind her lay the camp; ahead she could make out the gnarled trunk of a dead acacia, its limbs clutching the sky like the fingers of an arthritic hand. Beyond the tree lay the well, a dry hole marked by a cairn of stones.

Near the cairn she could see the two young lovers. They were locked in a tender embrace, blind and deaf to everything but each other. A turbaned shadow moved behind them. Then another and another. Raising the pistol, Megan cocked it and aimed. Time slowed as her finger tightened on the trigger.

Before she could fire, a huge, sweaty hand clamped over her mouth. Pain shot up her arm as the pistol was wrenched away. She tried to fight, twisting and scratching, but her captor was a wall of muscle. Powerless to move or cry out, she could only watch in horror as a knife sang out of the darkness and buried itself to the hilt in Gamal's back. He dropped without a sound.

Saida's screams shattered the darkness as the Janjaweed moved in. One of them flung her to the ground. Two others pinned her legs as the circle of men closed around her. Megan heard the sound of ripping cloth. Again Saida screamed. Again and again…

Megan's eyes jerked open. She was shaking violently, her skin drenched in sweat beneath her light cotton pajamas. Her heart slammed in the silence of the room.

Easing her feet to the floor, she brushed aside the mosquito netting, leaned over her knees and buried her face in her hands. The dream always ended the same way. She had no memory of how she'd managed to escape. She only knew that Gamal had been found dead outside the camp the next morning, and Saida had vanished without a trace.

She'd soldiered on, hoping time would help her forget. But even here in Arusha the nightmares were getting worse, not better. Maybe Dr. Musa was right. Maybe she did have post-traumatic stress. But so what if she did? As far as she knew, there was no simple cure for the malady. Otherwise, why would so many combat veterans be suffering from it back in the States?

All she could do was go on as if nothing had happened. If she could control her fears, she could still do some good. One day she might even be able to live a normal life.

But normal in every respect? She shook her head. That would be asking too much.

* * *

Wednesday was vaccination day at the clinic. While the aide managed the paperwork, and Dr. Musa took care of the more urgent cases, Megan spent the hours giving immunizations. Most of her patients, babies and children, had departed squalling. She loved the little ones and was grateful for the chance to help them stay well; but by late afternoon she'd developed a pounding headache.

Taking a break as the stream of people thinned, she gulped down a couple of aspirins. She couldn't help wondering where Cal was. He'd promised to come by the clinic, but she hadn't seen him for two days. Had some emergency come up, or was he just avoiding her?

But why should she care? Cal wanted to stir up memories she would be happy to keep buried. Seeing him again would only sharpen the loss that had dulled over time.

Dared she believe he'd given up on her and left? But that wasn't like Cal. He'd come here seeking satisfaction, and he wouldn't walk away without it. Was it just the money? Or was he looking for some closure in the matter of Nick's death? Either way, he was wasting his time. She had no insight to offer him.

But her conflict over the prospect of spending time with him went deeper than that.

The other night when the calming strength of his arms had temporarily eased her panic, she'd been grateful for his comfort—and troubled by how it made her feel. Cal was a compelling man, and he'd touched her in a way that had sent an unmistakable message. There was a time when she would have found him hard to resist. But when he'd held her so close that his arousal had hardened against her belly, it had been all she could do to keep from pushing him away and running off into the rain. Only when he'd stepped back had she felt safe once more.

Over the past months, it was as if something had died in her. The things she'd witnessed had numbed her to the point where she doubted her ability to respond as a woman.

The issue had come to light a few months ago when a volunteer MSF doctor in one of the camps had invited her for a private supper. He'd been attractive enough, and Megan had harbored no illusions about what to expect. Such things were common enough between volunteers, and though she'd never indulged before, she'd actually looked forward to a few hours of forgetting the wretched conditions outside. But when he'd kissed her, she'd felt little more than a vague unease. She'd tried to behave as if everything was all right; but as his caresses grew more intimate, her discomfort had spiraled into panic. In the end she'd twisted away, plunged out of the tent and fled with his words echoing in her ears— *What the hell's the matter with you? Are you frigid?*

By the next night the doctor had found a more agreeable partner. Megan hadn't attempted intimacy again. She'd hoped it had been a fluke, but her reaction to Cal had confirmed her suspicions.

Her problem hadn't gone away, and most likely wouldn't. If Cal had seduction in mind, the man was in for a letdown. For that, and for every other reason she could think of, it would be best if she never saw him again.

But that was not to be. The next morning, as Megan was eating a breakfast of scrambled eggs and coffee, he roared through the gate in an open jeep that bore the logo of one of the big safari companies. A flock of brown parrots exploded from the tulip tree as he pulled up to the bungalow.

Dr. Musa stepped out of the clinic, grinning as if in on some secret joke.

Cal vaulted out of the jeep. "Pack your things, Megan," he ordered. "You're coming with me—now."

"Have you lost your mind, Cal Jeffords?" She faced him on the porch steps, her arms folded across her chest. "What gives you the right to come in here and order me around as if I were six years old?"

His eyes narrowed, glinting like granite over a sharklike smirk. "I'm the head of the J-COR Foundation and you're a volunteer. Right now I'm volunteering you to come with me on safari for ten days. I've already cleared it with Dr. Musa." He glanced toward the doctor, who nodded. "Your replacement's flying in this afternoon, so the clinic won't be shorthanded. Everything's been arranged."

"And I have no say in any of this?"

"Dr. Musa agrees with me that your work here isn't giving you enough rest. You need a real break. That's what I'm offering you."

"Offering? Does that mean I can refuse?"

"Not if you're smart." He stood his ground at the foot of the steps, his slate eyes level with hers.

"What if I say no? Will you haul me off by force?"

"If I have to." He didn't even blink, and she knew with absolute certainty that he wasn't bluffing. Once the man made up his mind, there'd be no moving him.

Not that the idea of a safari seemed so bad. It might even speed her recovery. But how was she going to survive ten days with Cal? Scrambling for a shred of control, she squared her jaw.

"Fine, I'll go with you on one condition. If I'm fit and rested by the end of the safari, I want to be sent back to Darfur."

One dark eyebrow twitched. "Are you sure that's a good idea?"

"Is it a good idea for any of those poor people who have nowhere else to go? It's where I'm most urgently needed.

And without that goal, I can't justify wasting ten days on a…vacation."

He scowled, then slowly nodded. "All right. But while we're on safari, you're on orders to relax and have a good time. That's the best medicine you can give yourself if you want to recover. And as you said yourself, you'll need to be fit and rested to return there."

She took a moment to study him, the jutting chin, the steely gaze. Cal Jeffords wasn't spending precious time and money on a safari just to help her get better. The next ten days would be a contest of wills. She would need to be on her guard the whole time.

"So, do we have a deal?" he demanded.

Megan turned toward the door of the bungalow. Pausing, she glanced back at him—long enough for him to see that she wasn't smiling. "It won't take me long to pack," she said. "The coffee's hot. Have some while you're waiting."

The single-engine Piper Cherokee circled the rim of the Ngorongoro crater, a place designated by *National Geographic* as one of the world's Living Edens. Cal had been here two or three times over the years and knew what to expect. He was more interested in watching Megan, who was seeing it for the first time.

As the pilot banked the plane, she pressed against the window, looking down at the grassy floor of the twelve-mile-wide caldera. "This is amazing," she murmured.

"It's all that's left of an ancient volcano that blew its top." Cal shifted comfortably into the role of guide. "Geologists who've done the math claim it was as big as Kilimanjaro. Can you believe that?"

Megan shook her head. She'd been quiet during the short flight, and Cal hadn't pressed her to talk. There'd be plenty of time for conversation later. He studied her finely chiseled profile against the glass. Even in sunglasses, with no makeup and wind-tousled hair, she was a beauty. No wonder Nick had been eager to give her anything she wanted.

"We could've driven here in less than a day," he said. "But I wanted your first view of the crater to be this one, from the air."

"It's breathtaking." She kept her gaze fixed on the landscape below. "Why is it so green down there? The rains have barely started."

"The crater has springs that keep it watered year-round. The animals living there don't have to migrate during the dry season."

"Will we see animals today?" Her voice held a childlike anticipation. Once Megan had resigned herself to going, she'd flung herself into the spirit of the safari. Despite his hidden agenda, and his long-nurtured distrust of her, Cal found himself enjoying, even sharing, her enthusiasm.

"That depends," he replied. "Harris Archibald, our guide, will be meeting the plane with our vehicle. Where we go will be mostly up to him. You'll enjoy Harris—at least, I hope you will. He's a relic of the old days, a real character. Be prepared—he's missing an arm and he'll tell you a dozen different stories about how he lost it. I've no idea which version is true."

He'd been lucky to hire Harris for this outing, Cal reflected. The old man usually guided trophy hunters, and his talent for it had him in high demand. But when Cal had called on him in Arusha, Harris had just had a client cancel. He'd been glad for the work, even though shepherding a photo safari had meant changing the arrangements he'd already made.

The old rogue swilled liquor, swore like a pirate and had been through four wives; but when it came to scouting game, he had the instincts of a bloodhound. There was no doubt he'd give Cal his money's worth.

"Will we be sleeping in tents tonight?" Megan asked as the plane veered away from the crater toward the open plain.

"You sound like a little girl on her first camping trip." Cal squelched the impulse to reach out and squeeze her shoulder. She seemed in high spirits this afternoon, but he sensed the frailty beneath her cheerful facade. Or was that an act? He'd have to remember to be on his guard against her. This was a woman used to wrapping men around her little finger.

"Wait and see," he said. "I want you to be surprised."

And she would be, he vowed. By the end of the next ten days, Megan would be well rested, well fed, well ravished and trusting enough to tell him anything.

The plane touched down on an airstrip that was little more than a game trail through the long grass. Cal swung to the ground, then reached up for Megan. Using his hand for balance, she climbed onto the low-mounted wing and jumped lightly to earth.

A cool wind, smelling of rain, teased her hair and ruffled the long grass. Far to the west, sooty clouds boiled over the horizon. Lightning flickered in the distant sky. Megan counted the seconds before the faint growl of thunder reached her ears. The rain was still several miles away, but it appeared to be moving fast. Their personal gear had been unloaded and the plane was turning around to take off ahead of the storm. If no one showed up to meet them, she and Cal would be left in the middle of nowhere with no shelter to protect them from the weather or the wildlife.

But there was no way she'd let Cal know how nervous

she was. Glancing over her shoulder, she flashed him a smile. "So our big adventure begins."

He wasn't fooled by her bravado. "Don't worry, Harris will be here," he said. "The old boy hasn't lost a client yet."

As if his words were prophetic, Megan saw a mottled tan shape approaching in the distance. Lumbering closer, it materialized into a mud-spattered heavy-duty Land Rover with open sides and a canvas top. There were two men in the front seat—a tall African driver and a stockier figure in khakis and a pith helmet.

Waving to the pair in the Land Rover, the pilot gunned his engine. The little plane droned down the makeshift runway, cleared the ground and soared into the darkening sky.

Cal hefted the duffel bags and strode toward the vehicle, where he tossed the gear in the back, keeping hold only of the case he had told Megan held the binoculars and cameras. Once the bags were arranged, he opened the door for Megan to climb into the rear seat. The driver gazed politely ahead, but their aging guide turned around to give Megan a look that could have gotten him slapped if he'd been a generation younger.

The man reminded Megan of an aging Ernest Hemingway, with battered features that would have been handsome in his youth. His bristling eyebrows and scruffy gray beard showed lingering traces of russet. His blue eyes held a secretive twinkle that put Megan at ease.

"I'll be damned, Cal." He spoke with a trace of lower-class British accent. "You told me you were bringing a lady friend, but you didn't tell me how classy she was. Now I'll have to be on my best behavior."

Cal settled himself on the backseat. "Megan, my friend Harris Archibald needs no introduction," he said. "Harris, this is Ms. Megan Cardston."

"It's a pleasure to meet you, Mr. Archibald." Megan extended her hand, then noticed, to her embarrassment, the pinned-up right sleeve of his khaki shirt.

He chuckled and accepted her handshake from the left. "You can call me Harris. I don't hold much with formality."

"But I'm holding you to your remark about being on your best behavior, Harris," Cal said.

"Oh, you needn't worry on that account. I've long since learned my lesson about fooling around with the client's womenfolk. See this?" He nodded toward the stump of his arm, which appeared to have been severed just above the elbow. "Jealous husband with a big gun and a bad aim."

Cal rolled his eyes heavenward. Remembering what he'd told her about Harris's stories, Megan suppressed a smile. "And our driver?" she asked. "Are you going to introduce him?"

Harris looked slightly startled, as if most clients tended to ignore the African staff. "Gideon," he said. "Gideon Mkaba. We'll be in good hands with him."

"*Hujambo,* Gideon." Megan extended her hand over the back of the seat.

"*Sijambo.*" The driver smiled and shook her hand.

"So where are we going, Harris?" Cal broke the beat of awkward silence.

The guide grinned. "Thought you'd never ask! Elephant! Whole bloody herd of 'em down by the riverbed. We were scouting 'em when we saw your plane."

As the engine coughed to a rumbling start, lightning cracked across the sky with a deafening boom. The roiling clouds let loose a gush of water that deluged down on the vehicle's canvas top. Wind blew the rain sideways, dousing the passengers.

"Move it, Gideon!" Harris shouted above the storm. "They won't be there forever!"

"But it's raining!" Megan protested, shivering in her wet clothes.

Twisting in the front seat, Harris shot her a devilish grin. "Excuse me, miss, but the elephants don't bloody care!"

Four

By the time they came within sight of the riverbed, Cal had managed to clamber into the back of the jouncing Land Rover and find Megan's duffel among the gear. Pulling out her rain poncho, he reached over the seat, tugged it past her head and worked it down around her shivering body. It was too late to keep her dry, but at least the plastic sheeting would act as a windbreaker and help keep her warm.

As he moved back to the seat, she looked up at him. Her lips moved in silent thanks. A freshet of tenderness welled inside him. Even a strong woman like Megan needed someone to care about her. Something told him she hadn't had anyone like that in a long time.

But he hadn't come on this trip to feel sorry for her. He couldn't let sympathy—or any other emotion—divert him from his purpose.

"There." On a slight rise above the riverbank, Harris motioned for the driver to stop. The growl of the engine dropped to a low idle. Glancing back at Cal and Megan, the guide touched a finger to his lips and pointed.

At first Cal saw nothing. Then, not fifty yards ahead, a huge, gray silhouette emerged through the sheeting rain. Then another and another.

Cal could feel Megan's hand gripping his arm as the herd ambled toward them on silent feet. Did the tension in her come from awe or worry? He wasn't quite sure what to feel, himself. He knew that most animals in the game parks were accustomed to vehicles. But these elephants were close, and the open Land Rover offered little in the way of protection. He could only hope that Harris knew what he was doing.

Somewhere below them, hidden by the high bank, was the rain-swollen river. Over the rush of water, Cal could hear the elephants. They were vocalizing in low-pitched rumbles, their tone relaxed, almost conversational. Gideon slipped the gearshift into Reverse, ready to back away at the first sign of trouble. Surely, by now, the herd was aware of them. But the elephants continued on, undisturbed.

The leader, most likely an older cow, was within a stone's throw of the vehicle's front grille when she turned aside and disappeared through an opening in the riverbank. The others followed her—adult females, half-grown teenagers and tiny newborn calves trailing like gray ghosts through the rain, down the slope toward the river. Megan's grip tightened. Cal could sense the emotion in her, the fear and the wonder. He resisted the impulse to take her hand. They had just shared an unforgettable moment. He didn't want to risk spoiling it.

The last elephant had made it down the bank to the water. The contented sounds of drinking and splashing drifted up from below. Harris nodded to the driver, who backed up the Land Rover, turned it around and headed back the way they'd come.

"You had me worried, there," Cal admitted. "Any one of those elephants could have charged us."

Harris chuckled. "No need to fret. I know that herd, and I knew they'd be thirsty. They always take the same path down to the river. As long as we didn't bother them, I was pretty sure they wouldn't pay us much heed."

Megan hadn't spoken. "Are you all right?" Cal asked her.

Her voice emerged as a nervous laugh. "Unbelievable," she breathed. "And we forgot to take pictures."

Cal could feel her trembling beneath the poncho, whether from cold or excitement, he couldn't be sure. But her green-flecked caramel eyes were glowing beneath the hood. It had been a good moment with Megan, the elephants and the rain, he mused; maybe the best moment he'd known in a long time. But he couldn't forget what he'd come to do.

Megan had expected that being on safari would involve roughing it in a tent. In her cold, wet condition, the luxury lodge on the outer slope of the Ngorongoro Crater came as a welcome surprise. Less welcome was the discovery that Harris had clearly misread her relationship with Cal. He had reserved just one bungalow for the two of them. With one bed.

"Don't worry. I'll take care of this." Cal stood beside her in the open doorway surveying the elegantly rustic quarters, decorated in native rugs, baskets and tapestries. "While you shower and change for dinner, I'll go talk to the manager. They're bound to have an extra room somewhere."

With the door locked behind him, Megan stripped

down and luxuriated in the hot, tiled shower stocked with lavender-scented soap and shampoo. It wouldn't be a good idea to get used to this, she lectured herself. In the camps, a bucket of cold water was often as good as she could get. Much of the time she'd had to make do with sponge baths, reminding herself that even that was better than most refugees had.

If she could move beyond the panic attacks and the nightmares, Cal had promised to send her back to Darfur. Ten days wasn't much time. But if she could relax and focus on getting well, it might make a difference.

She wanted to go back, needed to. Working among the poor and dispossessed had given her the only real sense of worth she had ever known—something she had craved after her world had collapsed under her feet.

In her naïveté, she hadn't learned about Nick's embezzlement of the charity funds until days before he'd shot himself. Between his death and his funeral, she'd done a world of soul-searching. For years, she'd taken it for granted that her husband was rich, and she'd spent accordingly. But how much of the stolen money had gone to support her extravagant lifestyle? Megan had no way of knowing. She had known, though, that while she couldn't return the money, she could at least make some restitution through her own service.

Cal's cold anger at the funeral and his threat to make her pay had startled her. Until then she hadn't realized that he blamed her for the theft and for his friend's suicide. Knowing that he would find some way to go after her legally and that she had no power to fight him had pushed her decision—she'd had no choice except to run far and fast, where Cal would never think to look for her.

Using her political connections and her knowledge of the J-COR Foundation, she'd managed to expedite the paperwork and lose herself in the ranks of volunteers. What surprised her was the fulfillment she'd found in working with the refugees. They had needed her—and in that need she'd found the hope of redemption.

She was proud of the work she'd done in Arusha, but she could do so much more in Darfur. She had to go back; and she couldn't let Cal stop her.

Megan had put on fresh clothes and was fluffing her short damp hair when she heard a knock on the door. She opened it to find Cal standing on the threshold with his duffel bag.

"No luck," he said. "They've got a big tour group coming in tonight, and everything will be full-up. I even asked about borrowing a cot. Nothing."

"Can you room with Harris?"

"Harris has a single bed in the main lodge. He'll probably come in drunk, and even when he's sober he snores like a steam calliope. I let him know about his mistake—the old rascal just grinned and told me to make the best of it."

He glanced around the bungalow, which, except for the bath, was all one L-shaped room. Near the window, a sofa and two armchairs were grouped around a coffee table. "Sorry. I'll be fine sleeping on the couch. I even have some sheets and an extra mosquito net they gave me at the desk."

Grin and bear it. Megan sighed as her gaze measured his looming height against the modest length of the sofa. "I may be a better fit for the couch myself. But I suppose we can work that out. Come on in. You'll want to clean up before dinner."

While Cal showered, Megan opened the camera bag and went over the instruction manual for the small digital camera Cal had bought her in Arusha. In the background, she could hear the splash and gurgle of running water as he sluiced his body—probably a very impressive body, she conceded. But she'd been married to Nick for five years; and working in the camps, she'd seen more than her share of nudity. If Cal were to walk out of the bathroom stark naked, she would do little more than shrug and look the other way.

The small intimacies of sharing a room didn't bother her. It was Cal's constant, looming presence that would take some getting used to.

The shower had stopped running. The door opened a few inches to let out the steam, but it appeared he was getting dressed in the bathroom. A few minutes later he stepped out, freshly shaven and combed, and dressed in clean jeans and a charcoal-gray sweater that matched his eyes. The clothes should have seemed casual, but something about his presence lent a rugged elegance to whatever he wore. She'd always noticed that.

Megan had done some needed shopping in Arusha before their departure, but she'd bought mostly plain khakis and T-shirts, a fleece jacket and a pair of sturdy boots, which she could take back to Darfur. Her one indulgence had been a colorful but practical jade-green scarf, which she'd knotted at her throat tonight. It was as dressed-up as she was going to get.

She surveyed him from head to toe. "You look like a page out of *GQ*."

He grinned. "And you look like Ingrid Bergman in *For Whom the Bell Tolls*. Shall we go to dinner?"

It was still raining, but there was a good-size umbrella in the room. Stepping out onto the terrace, Cal opened it and sheltered Megan while she locked the door. With rain a streaming curtain around them, they followed the brick walkway across the grounds to the dining room.

The lodge stood on an old coffee plantation, its original German owners exiled by the British, who'd taken over the country at the end of World War I. The trees, the gardens and some of the old buildings had been preserved and beautifully restored. A high brick wall around the property kept out prowling animals. Veiled by rain and twilight, memories of a forgotten world lingered in the shadows. It seemed so distant from any world she'd been used to—in America or in Africa—that it almost felt like a dream. She'd have to remind herself not to get lost in it. This wasn't a fairy tale, she was not a princess and Cal was no Prince Charming. He was a man with an agenda, and she would do well to keep that in mind.

Gideon would be sleeping and eating in the staff quarters; but Harris was waiting at their table in the dining room. Already glowing from the whiskey in his glass, he kept them riotously entertained through the five-course gourmet meal. Megan was grateful for his presence, which saved her from making awkward conversation with Cal. She found herself liking the old rogue, despite his proclivities for strong drink and colorful curses. Even when he flirted outrageously with her, she took it in the good humor it was meant to be.

"Join me in the bar for a nightcap?" He gave her a sly wink as their dessert plates were whisked away. "We might even invite that old sourpuss Cal along if he asks nicely."

"Thanks, but I can barely keep my eyes open now," Megan said, rising. "Of course, I can't speak for Cal. But I'll see you tomorrow morning."

The men had risen with her. "I'll excuse myself, too, Harris," Cal said. "It's been a long day, and I know you'll want to get an early start in the morning."

"Where will we be going?" Megan asked.

"Wait and see," Cal teased. "More fun that way."

"Fine, but can you at least tell me where we are now? I've totally lost my bearings."

"Sure. I've got a map of the country in my bag. That'll give you a better idea."

They stepped outside to discover that the rain had stopped. The clouds had swept away to reveal a dazzling expanse of stars. Water dripped from the trees as they walked back down the path to their bungalow.

"How early does Harris expect us tomorrow?" Megan asked.

"Six, maybe. Early morning's the best time to see animals. He may be up half the night drinking, but don't worry, he'll be there first thing. And we'll be there, too, if we know what's good for us."

"You seem to know Harris pretty well. How did you meet him?"

"Partly luck. A few years ago I took one of our big donors to see some projects in Africa. The man was a hunter and wanted a safari while he was here. Harris was available."

"You hunted with them?"

"I just went along for the ride. Took a few pictures. Harris thought I was a wuss. Probably still does, but we managed to become friends. I've sent him other clients over the years, but after seeing those beautiful animals go down under the gun, I've no desire to hunt anything. Life's too short and too precious."

"I like that about you," Megan said, meaning it. "And I never thanked you for commandeering me on this trip. So far it's been wonderful."

She waited, expecting some kind of response, but Cal was silent. He hadn't brought her along on this trip for pleasure, Megan reminded herself. Or if he had, it was only because he thought that he could get her guard down and pry away her secrets.

Two years ago, Cal had been the one to walk into Nick's

office and find him dead at his desk. A shock like that would leave a lasting scar. If Cal had blamed her, even in part, for his best friend's suicide, the blame would still be there, festering like an infected wound beneath the veneer of charm and affability he was showing her now. Even before Nick's suicide, he'd never approved of her. He must hate her now.

Had he come here to punish her? Maybe she should simply ask him. She doubted he'd tell her the truth. Worse, voicing her suspicions might raise his guard. But at least it would let him know he wasn't fooling her.

"I've been thinking about our sleeping arrangement," she said. "If you try to stretch out on that sofa, you'll hang over the ends and keep us both awake with your tossing and turning. But I'm short enough to fit—not to mention the fact that, after living in the camps, I can sleep anywhere. You're taking the bed. End of discussion."

"Fine," he answered after a beat of silence. "I bow to your common sense. But you get one of the pillows and your first choice of blankets."

"Deal." They'd reached the terrace of their bungalow. She fished in her pocket for the key. "How long will we be staying here? Surely you can tell me that much without spoiling any surprises."

"We'll be using this lodge as our base for the next few days, so you can go ahead and unpack for now. After that... you'll see."

"Sorry, but I've grown accustomed to being in charge of my life."

"For the next nine days, your only responsibility will be to relax. Leave the logistics to Harris. That's what I'm paying him for."

"And what are *you* getting out of this?"

The slight intake of his breath told her that her question

had thrown him. In the silence that followed, she turned the key in the lock and opened the door. Before she could step inside, he touched her arm. "It's early yet. Let's sit outside for a while. If you think you'll be cold, I'll get a blanket."

"Thanks." The overhanging roof had kept the rain off the bench under the window, but the night breeze carried a chill. Megan took a seat, huddling for warmth while Cal went inside and turned on a lamp. He hadn't answered her question, but at least he seemed willing to talk.

Moments later he returned with a light woolen blanket. It was long enough to cover them both as he sat next to her. Megan was acutely conscious of his body heat and the rain-fresh aroma of his skin. She'd always found Cal intimidating, like facing down a lion. There was something about him that shriveled her self-confidence. It had gotten much worse after Nick's death, when he'd begun to treat her as an adversary. But she'd have to put her discomfort aside if she wanted him to deal with her as an equal.

The night was still except for the lightly rustling wind and the drip of water off the leaves and buildings. A night bird called from outside the wall, a shimmering sound that, in Megan, touched a chord of sadness.

"You asked me a question," Cal said.

Her heart stumbled. "I did. You don't owe me anything, Cal. You've no reason to like me, or do me any sort of kindness. For all I know, you still blame me for Nick's death. So why should you invest your time and money in this adventure? That's why I'm asking, what's in it for you?"

He stirred beside her. "Peace of mind, maybe. Or at least some answers. I've never gotten past what happened with Nick, or his death. For years he was my closest friend. I thought I knew him. But it appears I didn't know him at all. I want to move on. But for that, I need to understand

Nick and what motivated him to kill himself. I need to see
him through your eyes."

Megan swallowed the ache in her throat. As expected,
he hadn't asked her about the money directly. But his words
had stirred up some painful emotions. She'd asked for this;
but even after two years she wasn't ready to talk about
her marriage.

"I don't know if I can help you," she said. "When the
theft was discovered and Nick took his own life, I was as
shocked as you were."

"So have you been able to move on, Megan?"

Had she? Megan struggled with the question. She'd dealt
with Nick's death by running away to a part of the world
where tragedy was commonplace. But the past was still
there, like an unhealed wound, and now Cal wanted to rip
that wound open.

"Maybe we can help each other," he said. "It might do
us both good to talk."

"Talk about Nick?" She shook her head. "If that's what
you want from me, you've come a long way for nothing.
It still hurts too much."

Turning away from her, he fixed his gaze on the night
sky. Megan studied his craggy profile, the Roman nose,
the determined chin, as she waited to see how he'd respond
to her refusal of his request. Cal Jeffords wasn't a man to
take no for an answer.

"If talking about Nick's too painful, why don't you tell
me about yourself?" he persisted. "I don't know much
about your background, except that you were a nurse.
Where did you grow up, Megan?"

Even talking about her early life was hard. But Cal
wasn't about to let up. "I grew up in Arkansas," she said,
"in a little hill town you've never heard of."

He looked at her again, one eyebrow quirked. "I'd never have guessed it. You don't sound like a Southerner."

"I was born in Chicago and lived there till I was six. Then my parents died in a car accident—New Year's Eve, drunk driver, no insurance."

"Sorry. Tough break for a kid."

"My grandmother agreed to take me and raise me up 'in righteousness,' as she was fond of saying. Granny was a good woman, and she meant well, but…"

The words trailed off as Megan remembered the spankings with a hickory rod, meant to drive out the devil, the long passages of scripture learned by rote, the endless hours of sitting on a hard bench in revival meetings while the preacher raged hellfire and damnation.

"I get the picture," Cal said. "And I'm guessing some of that so-called righteousness was a hard pill to swallow right after losing your parents. No kid wants to be told that her parents had to die so they could be in a better place without her. It explains, in part, why you left that all behind so completely."

"Don't try to psychoanalyze me, Cal. I've done enough of that on my own."

"Fine. Go on." He shifted beneath the blanket, his knee brushing hers. Megan sensed a shift in his manner, but she willed herself to ignore it.

"We were so poor that we wore clothes from the church's charity bin. But Granny had inherited her little house and the acre of land it sat on. When I was seventeen, she died of a heart attack and left it to me. I sold the property to pay for college and never looked back."

"And so you became an angel of mercy." His tone was razor-edged. But given the extravagant way she'd lived with Nick, Megan could hardly blame him for being cynical.

"Oh, at first I had some idealistic dreams about what I

could do with a nursing degree," she said. "But by graduation I was broke, and the top-paying job I could find was with one of San Francisco's best-known plastic surgeons."

"I take it the good doctor didn't hire ugly nurses."

"That's not fair!" Megan reined the impulse to slap him. Apparently he'd dropped the pretense of just wanting to know her better. Now he was firmly back into judgmental mode—the way he usually was when he spoke to her, back before Nick's death. Their interactions had been limited, but his tone with her had always made his disdain perfectly clear.

"I was good at my work—very good," she insisted. "But yes, we had to project the right image for the clients—hair, makeup, fitted uniforms, the whole package. And I didn't mind. After years of donated clothes—washed out, shapeless and worn down nearly to rags—I enjoyed having nice things that I could buy new, and money to spend on a hairdresser or a manicurist. I learned a lot from the women who came in for procedures—where to shop, how to dress, where to get my hair done. Some of them were even friendly enough to invite me to their charity galas. That was how I met Nick." She paused, sensing she'd stepped onto dangerous ground. "That's it. You know the rest of the story."

"Yes. Cinderella went to the ball, met her handsome prince and they lived happily ever after…or, whatever the hell really happened."

The anger that flashed through Megan was as instantaneous as torched gasoline. She'd tried to be patient and open with the man. But he'd repaid her with sarcasm and contempt. Twisting on the bench, she faced him with blazing eyes.

"It's my turn to ask the questions, Cal Jeffords!" She flung the words at him. "I didn't steal the money! I didn't

kill Nick! I've done nothing immoral or illegal! What gives
you the right to be my judge and jury? What have I done
to make you hate me so much?"

"Hate you? Damn it, Megan, all I want is to understand what happened—and to understand you! Why do
you make it so hard?"

"You're the one who's making it hard," she flung back
at him. "You didn't come here for a good time. You came
because you wanted something. Why can't you just be
honest with me for a change? What kind of game are you
playing?"

With a muttered curse, he seized her shoulders and
jerked her close. For an instant his eyes burned their anguish into her soul. Then his mouth captured hers in a
brutal, crushing kiss.

Five

The heat of Cal's kiss jolted through Megan like the burn of a bullet. She felt a rush of sensation—too sharply intense for her to decide if it was even pleasurable or not. Then her pulse went crazy as stark panic set in. Wild with senseless fear, she thrashed against him, fists flying at whatever target they could find.

Shoving her to arm's length, he released her and sank against the back of the bench. His face reflected shock— and a few red marks from where her wild blows had connected—but he spoke calmly. "Megan, it's all right. Nobody's going to hurt you."

Something in his voice reached her. She willed herself to clasp her hands in her lap and breathe. She was safe, she told herself firmly. Cal hadn't meant to harm her. The only danger was in her mind.

As the panic ebbed, she began to tremble. Her shoulders sagged. Her head dropped into her open hands. How could she have let this happen?

"Forgive me, Megan. I should have known better." He made no effort to touch her; but when she found the courage to look up, his stricken eyes met hers. With wrenching effort, she found her voice.

"Please...I'll be fine. Just don't do that again," she whispered.

Releasing a long breath, he stood. "Relax. I'll get you something to drink." Stepping inside, he returned a moment later with one of the water bottles from the room and held it out to her. Megan took long sips, letting the cool water calm her. Her senses took in the fresh smell of rain and the musical drone of crickets in the darkness as her heartbeat calmed enough for her to hear past its thudding in her ears.

"Better?" he asked.

She managed to nod. "Getting there. Not quite the reaction you get from most of the ladies you kiss, is it? But I'm in no mood to offer any sort of apology. You were out of line. What were you thinking?"

"I won't even try to answer that question." His chuckle sounded strained. "Is there anything I can get you?"

"Not really. But some time alone to settle my nerves might help."

"Fine. I'll go keep Harris company in the bar. You won't be going anywhere else, will you?"

"Just to bed." The panic attack had drained her. She barely had the energy to speak. "Take the key. With luck I'll be asleep when you get back."

"Got it." His voice was edged with caution. "Rest, now. We've got a long day ahead of us tomorrow. Let's put tonight behind us and make it a good one." He turned to go, then glanced back at her. "I've learned my lesson, Megan. You have my word. I won't frighten you like that again.

You're right that you don't owe me an apology—I owe you one. I'm truly sorry for upsetting you."

Unable to form a response, she looked away and heard his footsteps fade around the corner of the bungalow. Outwardly she was calm enough. But Cal's kiss had set off a maelstrom of inner turmoil. Wrapping herself in the blanket, she struggled to sort out her thoughts.

Cal was experienced enough to read most women. If he'd had any idea she might fight him, he would never have kissed her. Had he picked up on signals she wasn't even aware of sending? Had she actually *wanted* to be kissed? By him, of all people? He was an attractive man, but she could honestly say she'd never imagined him in an intimate context. He'd always seemed so cold toward her—coldly disdainful at first, and then, at Nick's funeral, coldly vengeful.

She recalled, in vivid detail, the white-hot sensation that had flashed through her body as his lips crushed hers. There had been nothing cold about him in that moment. With the last man she'd kissed—the doctor in the camp—she'd felt nothing. With Cal, what she'd felt was a sensual overload so powerful it had terrified her.

What did it mean? Was she healing or getting worse?

What would happen if she let him kiss her again?

Trembling, she hugged her arms against her ribs. For now there was little chance of that. Cal had promised to leave her alone for the rest of the trip. If she was wise, she would hold him to that promise. The boundaries they'd set tonight were meant to keep her safe. Pushing those boundaries would involve more risk than she had the courage to take.

But there was one thing tonight had taught her. Cal wasn't the problem. She was.

Rising, she walked into the bungalow, locked the door and set herself to making her bed on the sofa.

Cal was in no frame of mind to sit around in the bar. His restless pace carried him along the darkened walkways, through the coffee grove and around the inside perimeter of the wall. With each stride, his thoughts churned.

He hadn't planned on kissing Megan. In fact, he'd warned himself not to. But it had happened—and the brief seconds it lasted had only sharpened his appetite for more. Even after her fear-driven response, his body ached with the desire to sweep her into bed and pleasure her torment away.

But never mind his own needs. There were darker forces at work here, and deeper concerns.

Megan's frenzied reaction had opened his eyes to what he should have realized earlier. She wasn't just exhausted from her time in the camps. And she wasn't just traumatized by the things she'd witnessed.

Something had happened to her.

Lack of cell service rendered Cal's mobile device useless here. But the lodge had a bank of antiquated computers with internet available for guests. Sitting in an empty spot, he logged in to his email and checked a few incoming messages, then opened a new window. Taking his time, he composed a message to the director in charge of volunteer records for the J-COR Foundation, requesting a copy of Megan's performance evaluations and medical history for the past two years. The records were supposed to be confidential; but as the foundation's head, he had the power to override that rule.

Megan would be upset if she knew he was meddling. But he needed to get to the root of her fear. Otherwise, how could he hope to understand her, or get her some help? Whatever their past connection, he could tell she was deeply troubled. How could he be so callous as to turn his back and leave her hurting?

He'd come to Africa with one purpose—to track down Megan and get justice for the loss of the money and Nick's death. But he hadn't counted on the complications. He hadn't counted on Megan's fragility or on his own accursed need to rescue the woman. He hadn't counted on becoming emotionally involved.

Now he was scrambling for answers—answers to questions he wouldn't have thought to ask a week ago. And it wasn't in his nature to walk away. He wouldn't rest, he knew, until he'd learned everything he needed to know about her.

Megan heard Cal come in and lock the door; but she pretended to be asleep. As his footsteps paused beside the sofa, she willed herself to keep perfectly still. She knew that he was no threat to her safety. But he might want to talk—and the last thing she'd wanted was to be grilled about what had happened tonight. Cal wasn't her doctor or her therapist. The mess inside her head was her private concern. She would deal with it in her own time, in her own way.

Before long, he was asleep in bed, snoring lightly. She lay awake in the darkness, comforted by the peaceful, masculine sound. Strange, how safe that sound made her feel.

If only she'd felt that way in his arms.

But Cal was a complication she didn't need right now. She was too damaged for any kind of relationship—especially with a man whose past history with her was one big red flag.

She was beginning to drift. The couch wasn't the most comfortable bed, but she'd slept on far worse; and the long day had worn her out. She'd come here to rest, she reminded herself; to relax and do her best to heal…if only she could.

For a time she slumbered quietly. Then, the specter rose from the darkness of sleep once more. Like bones exposed by blowing sand, it emerged, took shape, took on life and substance to become living memory. Once again she heard Saida's cry as her young lover fell. She saw the shadowy forms close around the helpless girl, heard the rough laughter as they flung her to the ground, heard the helpless cries and the sound of tearing cloth. Beyond the dry well, Megan writhed against the sinewy arms that held her, screaming into the greasy palm that clamped her mouth. She could smell the sweat, taste it…

Something jolted Cal awake. He sat up, eyes staring into the darkness. As his senses cleared, he heard muffled whimpers and the sound of thrashing from the couch.

Flinging the covers aside, he switched on a bedside lamp and stumbled out of bed. As he neared Megan, he saw that she'd become tangled in a web of netting and covers. Eyes closed in sleep, she was fighting to get free.

"Megan." He spoke softly, knowing better than to grab her or shake her. "Megan, wake up. You're dreaming."

Clearly in torment, she continued to struggle. Working with care, he pulled away the netting and the twisted sheet and blanket. It seemed to make a difference, ending her frantic writhing—though her expression remained tense and fearful. She sprawled in her cotton pajamas, calmer now as he bent over her. Daring to touch her, he smoothed the damp curls back from her forehead. "It's all right," he murmured. "You're safe. I'm here."

Her eyelids fluttered open. She stared up at him. "Cal?"

"You were dreaming. Do you know where you are?"

He saw the flicker of uncertainty in her eyes. "You're in the bungalow with me," he said. "Everything's all right."

Her breath came in hiccupping, dry sobs. Cal remembered her panic attack in the hotel, when she'd allowed him to draw her close. It had helped her then. But after she'd fought her way out of their kiss, he knew better than to reach out to her without her permission. "Would you like me to hold you?" he asked.

She hesitated, then nodded. Ever so gently he circled her with his arms, pulling her against his chest. She clung to him like a frightened child, her heart still hammering her ribs.

Megan, Megan, what frightened you so? What can I do to help?

This was no time to voice his questions. Maybe the medical report would tell him something. Until then, he could only do his best to comfort her.

The room was chilly. A glance at the clock confirmed that it was too early to get up. But he didn't want to risk leaving her alone on the couch. There was only one thing to do.

"Let me carry you to the bed," he said. "You'll be safe there, even from me, I promise. All right?"

When she didn't answer he lifted her in his arms. Her hands crept onto his shoulders as he carried her across the floor. Parting the mosquito net, he lowered her to the mattress and pulled the covers over her. She was still quivering when he left her to walk around the bed and switch off the lamp.

Could he really climb between the sheets with this woman and keep the promise he'd made to her? He didn't entirely trust himself awake, let alone half-asleep. But there was a precaution he could take.

Lifting the blankets, he slipped under them, leaving

the top sheet as a discreet layer between his body and Megan's. He couldn't recall ever sharing a woman's bed without planning to make love to her. But there was a first time for everything.

She lay curled slightly away from him, but he could feel her trembling body through the sheet. She couldn't possibly be asleep. "Are you all right?" he asked her.

"I will be."

"Tell me about your dream." Was he pushing her too fast? He wasn't sure she'd answer, but after a slow, unraveling breath, she spoke.

"There was this young girl who used to help me, when I was in Darfur. She was just fifteen, a beautiful child. She left the camp at night to meet a boy. I went after them, but I was too late."

"They were killed?"

"The boy was killed. The girl was…raped. Afterward she was never found."

"Janjaweed?"

"Yes."

"And you saw it happen."

"There was nothing I could do."

"I'm sorry, Megan." Acting on instinct, he laid an arm across her shoulders, on top of the covers. He half expected her to pull away, but the weight seemed to calm her. She was no longer trembling. Encouraged, he tightened his clasp. With a sleepy murmur she snuggled against him, warm through the sheet. "Go to sleep," he murmured. "No more bad dreams. I'm here."

She relaxed with a sigh, the cadence of her breath deepening. Wide-awake now, Cal lay holding her in the darkness. He had nothing but admiration for the volunteers who served in the refugee camps. The work demanded courage, compassion and the strength to look death in the face. Until Harlan Crandall's report, he would never have believed Megan capable of such fortitude. But her time in the camps had taken its toll. He'd seen evidence of that toll tonight.

He was familiar with the Janjaweed, of course—mercenaries paid by the Sudanese government for the express purpose of genocide against the black African population. Known as Devil Riders for the horses and camels they rode, they swept down on innocent civilians, killing, robbing and raping. Now that much of the bloody work was done, groups of Janjaweed had turned to banditry, even going so far as to rob the big white U.N. trucks that carried food and supplies to the camps. The refugees had little worth stealing, but if the marauders happened to catch an unguarded woman…

Cal's arm curled protectively around Megan's slumbering body. He could scarcely imagine the bravery it must have taken for her to go after that young girl and boy in the dark of night. At least she'd made it safely back to the camp. Thank heaven for that. Maybe now that she'd talked about the experience, she could begin the healing process.

She stirred, shifted and settled back into sleep. Now he could see the dark outline of her profile, fine-boned and elegant against the white pillowcase. His memory of the pampered ice queen he'd known in San Francisco was fading. This was Megan, as he thought of her now. And it was getting harder to reconcile her with the cold, high-living trophy wife whose extravagance had driven his best friend to suicide.

Cal had seen the checks himself—the generous donations from the charity events Megan oversaw that had never made it into the foundation's bank account. The graceful signature on the back had been Megan's, but they'd gone to a joint account in a different bank—an account in her name and Nick's. The online statements had gone to their home computer, which was registered to Megan. By the time the theft was discovered, the account had been almost empty.

How could he not believe she'd been involved in the theft, or even responsible for it?

Was there more to the story than what he knew? He wanted to believe that Nick was innocent—or that, at worst, he'd crossed the line solely to please his demanding wife. Nick had seemed so proud of her, so anxious to satisfy her every whim. But the woman beside him now didn't seem the type to manipulate her husband into theft—especially since the money had been earmarked for aid to the very same people she'd spent the past two years nursing.

Had Nick's death triggered a change of heart, making her regret her past actions? Had she changed…or had he been wrong about her all along?

Whatever was going on with Megan now, Cal couldn't let himself forget what had happened back in San Francisco. He'd been betrayed by the friend he would have trusted with his life. If he'd mistrusted Nick, how could he let himself believe that Nick's wife was blameless?

He couldn't afford to trust her until he knew the whole truth, no matter how ugly.

Megan woke alone in the bed. The bungalow was dark, but as her confusion cleared she became aware of water running in the bathroom. Beneath the closed door she could see a sliver of light.

Sitting up, she switched on the bedside lamp. Now she remembered the dream, and the aftermath—Cal's comforting voice, his strong arms lifting her off the couch and carrying her across the room to the bed. Amazingly, she'd slept for the rest of the night without nightmares.

She'd just flung back the covers when he stepped out of the bathroom, shaved, combed and dressed. He gave her an easy grin.

"Good morning, sleepyhead. I was about to wake you."

"What time is it?" she asked with a yawn.

"Five-thirty. Harris wants us on the road by six, so get a move on. There'll be coffee and a light breakfast in the lobby."

"Where are we going?" She dropped her feet to the cold tile floor.

"You'll see. It's a surprise."

"A surprise! Why do you and Harris insist on treating me like a five-year-old?"

His laughter followed her into the bathroom as she closed the door with a decisive click. She remembered what he'd said last night. Yes, it was time to put the drama behind her and start the day fresh.

By the time Gideon pulled the Land Rover up to the front of the lodge, Megan had finished her breakfast. The trees were alive with bird calls, and the amethyst sunrise promised clear weather. She looked forward to a day of adventure. Maybe this trip was exactly what she'd needed.

She stole a glance at Cal, where he stood talking with Harris. Her gaze traced the taper of his back from well-muscled shoulders to taut buttocks. By any measure, the man was prime stud material. But last night had proved she wasn't fit for any kind of physical relationship. Maybe she never would be.

At least he seemed to understand that. Since that disastrous kiss, he'd treated her like a kid sister. Even sharing the bed with him had been a chaste experience—perhaps a first for a man like Cal.

She tore her gaze away from his body. Under different conditions, she might not have minded sharing more than a blanket. But something vital in her was broken, shattered by forces she couldn't even name. If she was going to panic again, as she surely would, the last person she wanted it to happen with was Cal Jeffords.

"Ladies aboard!" Harris gave her a wink as he crushed his cigar with his boot heel and swung into the front passenger seat. "And may I add that you're looking right pert this morning, Miss Megan! Are you ready for your surprise?"

"Bring it on!" She tossed her day pack into the vehicle's bed, behind the backseat. It bounced off a basketball-size chunk of broken concrete lying next to the tailgate. "Is that what you plan to throw at anything that attacks us?" she joked.

"That's my wheel block," Harris said. "Believe me, if you get a puncture out there or need to park on a hill, you don't want to have to go looking for a rock. There could be some nasty surprises in that long grass. I've never had to use it—hope I never will. But it pays to be prepared."

Giving him a grin, she climbed into the backseat and spoke to the driver. "Good morning, Gideon. It's nice to have you with us."

"Thank you, miss." His tone was formal, but his expression told her he was pleased with her greeting.

"Let's go." Cal climbed into the backseat with Megan. The air was cool now, but the rising sun promised to be hot. Megan tightened the chin strap on her canvas hat. She was going to need it.

Cal studied Megan as the Land Rover climbed the winding road to the rim of the Ngorongoro Crater. She had just discovered where they were going today, and she was as excited as a child at the circus. Last night he'd feared for her mental state. But seeing her this morning, radiant and laughing, with her jade-green scarf knotted at her throat, was worth every dollar this safari had cost him. If he were meeting her for the first time today, with no past history between them, he could easily see himself falling for her charm.

This must have been the woman Nick saw when he looked at her. For the first time, Cal understood why Nick had fallen so hard and so fast. And Cal could no longer really say that he blamed him.

The thought shook him. Nick had been the type to fall in love easily, but while Cal had known plenty of women, he hadn't fancied himself in head over heels since high school. He'd been too serious, too driven for such frivolous emotion. He'd always felt that it was an advantage he had over Nick. But it didn't feel like too much of an advantage at the moment.

He put the thought out of his head. Megan was a fascinating package, but not what he'd call a candidate for a stable relationship. And he'd be a fool to let desire color his need for justice.

This morning he'd taken a moment to check his email. The medical report hadn't arrived. It might not arrive for days. Meanwhile he had no choice except to be patient—and Cal was not a patient man.

A flock of doves whooshed out of a flowering tree and soared skyward against the sunrise. "Beautiful…" The word was a whisper on Megan's lips. Cal remembered kissing those lips, crushing them with his. And he remembered what had followed. What had thrown her into panic? Was it him?

The Land Rover had crested the top of the crater and

was starting down the graveled road to the vast caldera below.

"Can you see any animals yet?" Cal asked Megan. "Here, take the binoculars."

Looking out the open side of the vehicle, she scanned the landscape below. "All I can see is grass and brush."

"You'll see a lot more when we get to the bottom," Harris said. "Last time I was here I saw a black rhino. Poor buggers will be extinct if the poachers get many more of them. The horns are worth big money. Arabs buy them for dagger handles. And powdered rhino horn's the rich Chinese version of Viagra. Works on the mind if nothing else, I suppose. Not that I've tried it—or needed to." He shot Cal and Megan a mischievous look.

"Are there poachers here in the crater?" Megan asked.

"They've been known to sneak in at night. Rangers have the go-ahead to shoot them on the spot. I'd do the same if I caught the bastards."

"But you guide hunters, don't you Harris?"

"Not here. This place is a national park. The animals here are meant to be protected. And legal hunting's not like poaching. Hunters pay thousands for a license to take one trophy animal. Part of the money goes to fund game management, including protection for animals like our rhino friend. And the cash that goes into the economy encourages the locals to see wild animals as the resource they are. Poaching's like the dark side. It takes all the good away."

"I see something." Cal pointed to a cluster of black dots. "Down there to the right, four o'clock."

Harris nodded. "Cape buffalo. Tough and mean as they come. We can get closer in the vehicle, but don't let them catch you on foot. I learned that lesson the hard way—see this?" He pointed to his empty, pinned-up sleeve. "Biggest bull you ever saw. Damn near killed me."

Lifting an eyebrow, Cal glanced at Megan. She rewarded him with a wink and a sexy smile that kicked his pulse into overdrive. He cursed silently. A few hot nights between the sheets would suit him fine. But with her panic attacks, her shadowed past and her connection to Nick and the stolen money, Megan was the last woman he should get serious with.

He could see it happening, and it made a delicious picture. Sharing some pillow talk with Megan had been his plan all along. But he hadn't planned on becoming emotionally involved. He was walking a fine line, and Lord help him if he stepped over. He could find himself in serious trouble.

Six

Megan gripped her camera, hesitant to raise it and risk triggering a charge. She'd heard how dangerous the huge black Cape buffalo could be. But these seemed accustomed to vehicles. They barely raised their massive heads as the Land Rover passed at a fifty-yard distance. Egrets—fairy white—stalked among their ebony legs, unafraid as they probed for insects in the grass.

"They seem so peaceful," she whispered to Cal. "And look, there's a little black calf—and another!"

"All the more reason to be careful." Cal's low voice was close to her ear. "They're family animals. Very protective."

"We should be seeing more babies." With the buffalo upwind of them, Harris spoke in his normal tone. "Now that the rains have started, there'll be plenty of grass— plenty of meat for the predators, as well. Good time to raise young ones."

Megan gazed ahead to an open plain where dainty

Thomson's gazelles were grazing. The ebony stripes along their sides glimmered in the morning sunlight.

"Do you have children, Harris?" she asked.

"A boy by my second wife. She took him home to England after the divorce. I hear he's a barrister of some sort, but we don't talk."

"I'm sorry."

"That's life, girl. You play the hand you're dealt and make the best of it."

Wise words, Megan thought. She'd been trying to make the best of her own life. But surprises kept throwing her off track. Surprises like Cal Jeffords showing up and turning her world upside down.

"How about you, Gideon?" she asked the driver. "Do you have a family?"

A smile broadened his long face. "Yes, miss. Three fine boys and two girls. They keep my wife very busy."

"I can tell you're very proud of them."

"Yes, miss. Good children are a blessing from God."

Something had spooked the gazelles. Their heads and tails shot up, and they burst into glorious flight, leaping and bounding like winged creatures. Even the little ones, all legs, were fleet enough to keep up with the herd as they vanished over a rise.

Gideon glanced at Harris, who nodded. "Lion, maybe. Come up easy."

Lion. Megan's heart crept into her throat as the Land Rover slowed to a crawl. She'd been in Africa for two years, but there were few, if any, large wild animals left in the places where she'd worked. Outside of a zoo, she'd never seen a lion.

In the open-sided vehicle, they were fully exposed to any creature that might decide to attack them. She'd glimpsed the high-powered rifle Harris kept mounted next to the passenger door, but he didn't seem concerned about having it ready.

She glanced at Cal. Reading her anxiety, he laid a light hand against her back. She moved closer to him. He might not be much use against a lion, but his size and strength made her feel safer.

The Land Rover inched around a bend in the narrow road, and suddenly there they were—two lionesses, sprawled on the grass a mere stone's throw away. The larger one studied the vehicle and its passengers with calm amber eyes. Her huge mouth opened in a disdainful yawn that showed yellowed fangs as long as Megan's fingers.

"Mother and daughter, I'd say," Harris whispered. "Look, the older one's pregnant. Big sister will likely stick around to help raise the cubs. Go ahead and take a picture. They're posing for you."

Megan's hands shook as she centered the pair in her viewfinder and pressed the shutter. The click was startling in the silence, but the lionesses barely glanced toward the sound. Gideon was about to move on when Harris touched his arm. "Hold it," he whispered. "Here comes papa!"

Megan was aware of a stirring, like wind in the long grass. She forgot to breathe as a majestic male lion strolled into view. Regal and unhurried, he seemed more interested in the females than in the Land Rover and the lowly humans inside. There was no need to prove who was king here.

Megan managed a few more shaky photos before Gideon pulled away, leaving the lions in peace. Harris grinned. "Now there's a life for you! The women raise the cubs and bring down the meat. Nothing for the old man to do but fight and make love."

"Not that he has it that easy." Cal's voice was close to

Megan's ear. "He has to defend his territory and his family from gangs of rival males. The stakes are life and death."

"That's a grim thought," Megan said. "Oh, look! Zebras out there in the open! And what's up there, next to the road? Something black!"

"Warthogs," Harris said. "A family of them, rooting for their breakfast."

"And they've got babies!" Megan rose in the seat, aiming her camera and snapping. "Look at them! So tiny and so cute!"

"Again, it's the male's job to protect them." Cal steadied her with a hand at her waist. "He may not be very big, but those tusks can rip a lion's belly, and the lions know it."

She glanced down at him. "Why aren't you taking pictures?"

He gave her his Hollywood grin. "I've got plenty of pictures from other trips. Right now I'm having more fun watching you."

Cal had spoken the truth. Being with Megan today was like being with a little girl at Disneyland. She was so natural and so excited; every minute with her was a delight.

He remembered the glittering ice queen who'd been married to Nick—perfect hair and makeup, runway clothes, the best of everything. Which one was the real her? Was this exuberance a part of her that she'd stifled all those years? If so, then he could almost understand Megan running away to escape the person she'd become.

What if it hadn't been about the money, after all? Today he could almost believe that. But no—he brought himself up short. Megan was as changeable as the wind. He'd be a fool to start trusting her.

Last night he'd watched her fall apart. Today she was behaving as if nothing had happened. Had the panic attack and the nightmare been some kind of performance, staged to gain his sympathy?

But how could that be? How could any person with a shred of honesty be capable of such deception? He couldn't believe that of Megan. But what *could* he believe about her? He had little choice except to wait for the report he'd ordered and hope it would give him some insight.

They stopped to eat bagged lunches on a safely fenced rise with primitive restrooms, picnic tables and a wide vista of the grassland below.

"I still can't believe one of those lions didn't jump right into our laps." Megan took a sip of her bottled water. "What would you do, Harris, if something like that happened?"

"I'd fire into the air and try to scare the bugger away. There'd be no end of trouble if I shot one of those babies in the park. Best way to keep that from happening is to read their body language. If they're looking uneasy, you keep your distance. Those lions we saw back there were as mellow as big pussycats. Otherwise we'd have given them a wide berth."

"Have you ever had an animal charge your vehicle?"

"Just once. White rhino in Tarangire. Made a bloody dent in the door and crushed my arm. That's how this happened." He glanced toward the pinned sleeve. Megan shot Cal a knowing glance, her eyes dancing, her smile a flash of white in her tanned face. He'd thought she was beautiful when she was married to Nick. Today she was spectacular.

The breeze had freshened. Harris squinted toward the far rim of the crater, where black clouds churned above the horizon, ready to stampede across the empty sky.

"We'd best be heading back," Harris said. "But there's plenty of time. We'll take a different road, off the beaten track as they say. Might see something new."

Megan climbed into the backseat and settled next to Cal. The morning had been incredible, but the hours spent in the hot sun and the jouncing, swaying vehicle had taken their toll. As time passed, her energy had begun to flag.

Back in the camps, she'd spent her days working in the infirmary from first light to bedtime, collapsing on her cot and then getting up at dawn to more of the same. Only now that she had the luxury of rest did Megan realize how exhausted she'd become. Even so, she missed being useful. When she got back to the bungalow, she would find some paper and write letters to people she'd known and worked with in the refugee camps. If she could let them know she meant to come back, that would strengthen her own resolve to get strong again.

After she finished the letters, maybe she'd look for some light reading in the lodge gift shop—a thriller or maybe a romance, anything to engage her mind and block the nightmares before she went to sleep.

The distant growl of thunder pulled her back to the present. Cal was watching her, mild concern in his eyes. "I thought you were about to nod off," he said.

"Would you have let me?"

"Only until we saw something you wouldn't want to miss. If you're sleepy, my shoulder makes a good pillow."

For an instant Megan was tempted. But accepting Cal's offer might be courting fate. Bad enough that Cal had witnessed one of her nightmares. She didn't want Harris or Gideon to see them, too. She shook her head. "I'm fine—and I don't want to miss anything."

The sky was getting darker now as fast-moving rain clouds blocked the sun. The Land Rover had cut off onto a side trail and was crossing an open plain dotted with thornbush. A herd of zebras and dark-hued wildebeest grazed in the distance. There were no other vehicles in sight.

"Along here is where I saw the black rhino," Harris said. "If he's still in the neighborhood, we might get lucky. Keep your eyes open."

He'd no sooner spoken than the sky split open as if someone had slashed a giant, water-filled balloon. Thunder roared across the horizon as sheets of gray rain turned the road to a quagmire of flowing mud.

Gideon muttered what Megan assumed to be a curse. Harris, however, was undeterred. "What's a little rain?" he shouted, grinning. "We can't stay here, so nothing to do but keep going!"

The canvas roof kept off the overhead downpour, but water was still blowing in. Megan, who hadn't thought to bring her rain poncho, was already drenched. There had to be a way to roll down the side covers. But she assumed it would involve stopping and having someone get out— impractical now because they'd just come up on another herd of Cape buffalo.

Something—maybe the lightning and thunder—had disturbed the hulking black beasts. More numerous than the first group, they were milling and snorting like range cattle on the verge of a stampede. Megan remembered Harris's words about reading an animal's body language. The signs that she could read from them made it clear that danger was very real.

The others seemed to agree. Gideon was driving as fast as he dared, trying to get past the herd without agitating them further. As the vehicle swayed along the muddy road, Megan found herself shivering, not only with cold but with fear.

Reaching across the seat, Cal circled her with his arm and drew her close. She huddled against his side. There was little warmth to be had, but she found the hard bulk of his body comforting, like a rock to cling to for safety.

What happened next happened fast. A low, dark shape—a warthog—shot across the road, almost under the front wheels. Instinctively, Gideon slammed the brake. The animal streaked away unharmed, but the Land Rover fishtailed in the thick mud and crunched to a stop with one rear wheel resting in a water-filled hole at the roadside.

Gideon revved the engine and tried to pull out—once, then again, rocking forward and back. It was no use. The mud was so slippery that the heavy-duty tires could find no purchase. They spun in place, shooting geysers of mud and water.

For a tension-filled moment nobody spoke. But Megan guessed what the men were thinking. The rain could go on for hours, making the road even worse. Even if they could radio for help, it was doubtful that anyone could get here before the storm let up. If they were going to free the vehicle, somebody would have to brave the buffalo and push from behind.

Since Gideon knew the vehicle best, it made sense for him to stay at the wheel. With one arm, Harris could neither push nor shift and drive efficiently. That left Cal—the huskiest of the men—to climb out into the mud.

The buffalo had turned as one to watch them. Frozen in place for the moment, they were perhaps fifty yards away—a distance that a charging animal could cover in a heartbeat.

Harris lifted the rifle from its bracket next to the door. "I'll cover you," he said. "If the bastards get any closer, I'll fire over their heads, try to scare them off."

Megan read the knowing glance the two men exchanged. If one of the massive bulls were to actually charge, there'd be little chance of stopping it, even if Harris aimed to kill. A single rifle shot, even a lucky one, wouldn't be enough to drop it on the spot. And a wounded Cape buffalo would be a murderous foe.

"Why not scare them off now?" Megan asked.

"Risky," Harris grunted. "Spooking them could make them more aggressive. Safest thing is to keep them calm, if we can."

"What can I do to help?"

"Pray," he snapped, dismissing her.

Harris shouldered the rifle with his left hand, resting the barrel on the door. Megan had wondered briefly whether he could handle a gun with one arm. Evidently he could.

He glanced back at Cal. "Whatever you do, keep your head down and stay close to the vehicle," he said. "If the buffalo see you in the open, you're in trouble. Ready?"

"Ready." Ducking low, Cal climbed into the back of the Land Rover and bellied over the tailgate. Megan's heart crawled into her throat as she watched him go. More than anything she wanted to stop him. Harris had told her to pray, but her mind had lost the words. There was nothing she could do but watch.

She could see the back of Cal's head and shoulders as he braced himself behind the rear bumper. "Hit it," he growled.

Gideon slammed the vehicle into gear and gunned the engine. The wheels inched forward, spattering mud, then the rear sank back into the hole.

Cal muttered a curse. "Can you back it out?"

"I already tried. No good," Gideon said.

"There's a shovel back here. Can we dig out a track?"

"Better not to try," Harris said. "That much activity could set off the buffalo." He was looking not at Cal but at the herd. As lightning crackled across the sky, they were becoming more agitated, stamping, lowing and tossing their heads. The biggest bull of all, with curling horns as broad and thick as the bumper on a truck, had moved front and center. His nostrils flared as he processed the alien odors of motor exhaust and human sweat.

Cal repositioned himself behind the tailgate. "All right. Again."

Once more the engine roared. Cal's shoulder muscles strained like steel cables as he pushed back and upward. The tires spun and spat showers of mud before he gave up and slumped forward. "We need something to brace that wheel." His voice rasped with fatigue. "A rock, maybe to jam in the hole."

A rock! Megan remembered the chunk of concrete she'd seen in the back of the truck. It might work, but Cal couldn't shove it in place while he was pushing. He would need a second pair of hands. Hers.

The buffalo were massing behind their leader. Rain poured down their sleek black sides and dripped off their horns. Megan forced herself to look away and concentrate on her task as she slipped into the back bed of the vehicle and found the concrete. Harris and Gideon were watching the herd. They hadn't noticed her, but Cal did.

"What in hell's name do you think you're doing?" His eyes blazed in his mud-coated face.

She hefted the gray chunk, which was even heavier than it looked. "Hold this," she hissed, passing it to him.

He took it, but when she started to scramble over the tailgate, his gaze narrowed dangerously. "For God's sake, Megan, stay put!" he growled.

"You need me." She dropped to the ground, staying close to the vehicle. Taking the piece of concrete from him, she knelt and set it rough-side-up against the back of the mired wheel. She tried not to think about the buffalo and how close that big bull might be. Rain soaked her hair and streamed down her body, but she no longer felt the chill.

"Tell Gideon to try it again," she said, hoping Cal had one more push left in him. He was a powerful man, but he was only human and the effort would be excruciating.

He positioned himself against the bumper, feet braced, eyes meeting hers through the gray veil of rain. "Be careful," he muttered. "This thing could roll back and crush your hand."

"I'll be fine."

"If there's a charge, roll under the vehicle. That'll be the safest place. Understand?"

She gave him a nod, willing herself not to look toward the buffalo. "Ready."

"Hit it!"

Gideon gunned the motor to a roar. Grunting with the strain, Cal pushed and lifted. Spitting showers of mud, the mired wheel inched forward, leaving just enough space and time for Megan to shove the lump of concrete into the hole.

But would it be enough? As she tumbled backward, out of the way, Cal eased off long enough to let the tire settle onto the solid surface. Gideon was still racing the engine. Now, finding slight purchase, the wheel began straining forward.

"Now!" Cal began pushing with all his might. Scrambling to her feet, Megan flung herself next to him. Her weight was scant, her strength meager, but coupled with his it might be enough to make a difference.

Inch by inch the Land Rover crept forward. Now it was out of the deep mud, moving forward onto the main trail and gaining speed. Harris was whooping like a cowboy on Saturday night.

Hoisting Megan in his arms, Cal dumped her over the tailgate and clambered after her. She sat up and swung her attention back to the buffalo. The bull had burst into a false charge but stopped short, snorting and tossing its horns in what could almost pass as a victory dance at the sight of their retreat.

Bracing her by the shoulders, Cal looked her up and down as if inspecting her for damage. His hat was gone, and he was coated with mud from his hair to his boots. Megan realized she must look the same. "You're all right?" he asked.

She gave him a grin. "Never better. We did it!"

"You crazy woman! You could've been killed!" He caught her close, holding her fiercely against his chest. She was dimly aware of Harris and Gideon in the front seat, but it was as if the two men were far away and nobody was here but Cal. Adrenaline rushed through her body. She felt wonderfully wild and reckless.

"You brave, beautiful fool!" Laughing, he cradled her close, muddy clothes and all. His arms were warm and safe, his laughter like a joyful drug. Carried away, Megan was surprised to find herself wanting to be kissed—really kissed—by him.

But there was no way Cal was going to kiss her. Not after what had happened the last time. If Megan wanted a kiss from him, there was only one thing she could do.

Fueled by euphoria, she hooked his neck with her arm, pulled him down to her and pressed her parted lips to his.

Seven

Megan sensed the shock of Cal's surprise. Her heart shrank as he stiffened against her. But he was quick to recover. With a little growl of laughter, he took charge. His compelling mouth molded to hers with a teasing flick of tongue—playful and, at the same time, so sensual that she experienced a delicious twinge at the apex of her thighs.

The fear was still there, slumbering in the depths of her awareness. But the thrill of Cal's kiss swept her away like a plunge over a waterfall. For a fleeting moment, she savored the sweetness of something she'd believed lost.

Too soon, he ended the contact. "We have an audience," he muttered in her ear.

Megan glanced forward to find Harris turned in his seat, grinning back at them. "I'll be damned," he said with a wink. "I knew you two would come around. All it took was a thunderstorm, a stuck wheel and a herd of buffalo."

"Eyes front, *mzee*," Cal said, using the Swahili term for

an old man. He smiled as he spoke, but Megan sensed that any more kissing would have to wait for a private time.

Riding in the bed of the Land Rover was rough and wet. Cal boosted her over the back of the seat and took his place beside her. His arm circled her shoulders, pulling her against his side to protect her from the worst of the storm.

Megan's heart hammered as she weighed the risky step she'd just taken. Had she turned a corner? Was she really getting better, or had the moment's excitement swept her away?

She yearned to be emotionally well again. To go through life unafraid of intimacy, to make love, even to remarry and have children—that was what she'd wanted all along. But over the past months she'd lost hope. The fear that had frozen some vital part of her—a fear so dark and deeply rooted that she didn't fully understand it herself—still lurked like a monster in its cave, waiting to reach out with its cold tentacles and crush her courage.

Back in America she might have sought professional help. But here what little help there was to be had was focused on treating the trauma of refugees—which was as it should be. And going home would only bring her up against the demons Nick's death had left behind.

For the first time she felt a glimmer of hope. She'd fought her attraction to Cal for as long as she'd known him. Now there was no more reason to fight. Something about his solid strength wrapped her in a sense of safety. His kiss had left her with a delicious buzz. But was it enough? Could she risk more, especially when she knew the reason he'd come here? Could she trust him not to manipulate her, or use her vulnerability against her? He'd been so good to her the previous night, but could she truly trust him? And could she trust herself not to get too invested?

Even if she dared go the distance, she knew better than

to think a fling with Cal would last. He wasn't the sort of
man to settle on one woman. Even if he was, his dark suspicions and the painful history they shared would drive
them apart. But he was an exciting man—a very sexy man.
And she had little doubt he'd be willing to cooperate with
her present needs.

Was it time she faced her fear?

The Land Rover crawled upward toward the rim of the
crater. The going was treacherous, with rain churning
the road to mud; but soon the long drive would be over.
Chilled to the bone, Cal looked forward to a hot shower,
dry clothes, a gourmet dinner at the lodge—and just maybe
something more.

Megan nestled against his side, the contact of their bodies providing the only spot of warmth. As his arm tightened around her shoulders, she glanced up and gave him
a quiet smile. She'd been amazing today, braving the buffalo to climb out of the vehicle and brace the wheel. How
many women—or men—would have shown that kind of
courage?

Her kiss, he suspected, had demanded a different kind
of courage. After last night's panicked response, her sweet
passion had caught him off guard. Whatever she'd meant
by it, he wasn't complaining. But now what?

Clearly Megan was up to something. But he knew better
than to push her. Be patient, Cal lectured himself. Let her
take the lead; then follow to where they both wanted to go.

Hadn't he meant to seduce her all along? If that was
what the woman had in mind, she was playing right into
his hands. Get her warm and purring, and maybe she'd
open up about what had happened in San Francisco.

It was still raining by the time they topped the crater and
made it downhill to the lodge. Gideon pulled up in front to

let his weary passengers climb out of the vehicle. Harris headed inside, probably for a warming glass of whiskey at the bar. Cal helped Megan out of the backseat. Chilled, muddy and cramped from sitting in the rain, they made their way down the brick path to their bungalow. They paused to leave their muddy boots on the doorstep for the staff. Then Megan used her key to open the door.

Inside, Cal fished a Tanzanian shilling out of his pocket. "I'll flip you for the first shower."

Meeting his eyes, she took the coin out of his hand. "It's a big shower," she said.

Cal was quick to get her meaning, even though her fingers trembled as she laid the coin on the table. This was her call, he reminded himself. All he had to do was follow her lead. He would have Megan right where he wanted her.

Their clothes were dripping mud. It didn't make sense to shed them anyplace but in the spacious, tiled shower, where they could at least rinse out the worst of the dirt. Megan walked into the bathroom, leaving the door open. Turning on the water, she stepped into the shower and began unfastening her mud-soaked blouse. Her quivering fingers fumbled with the buttons.

"Let me give you a hand." After shedding his leather belt, his watch and his wallet, Cal stepped in beside her and took over the buttons. He heard her breath catch as his knuckle brushed her breast. Slow and easy, he reminded himself. Megan was putting herself out to make this work. The last thing he wanted was to frighten her back into her shell.

Her jade-flecked eyes widened as the front of her blouse fell open to reveal a lacy black bra—perhaps a relic of the old days in San Francisco. The sight of that dark lace against creamy skin triggered an ache of raw need. Cal suppressed a groan as his sex rose and hardened. All he wanted right now was to rip off her wet clothes, sweep her into bed and bury himself inside her.

But haste could ruin everything. Megan was clearly willing to try. But he knew she'd been traumatized, and one wrong move could spoil everything. If he wanted her, he would have to hold back, be patient and let her set the pace.

If he could manage to keep himself under control.

Cal's shirt was open to his chest. Willing herself to stay calm, Megan freed the remaining buttons, down to the waistband of his trousers. There was nothing to be afraid of, she told herself. She'd been married to Nick for five years. Being naked with a man and having sex was nothing new. And she *wanted* this. She needed it. So why was her heart pounding like a jackhammer gone berserk?

She could feel his eyes, those perpetually cold gray eyes that had always seemed to look right through her. Eyes she remembered as contemptuous, especially after Nick's death. If she looked up, what would she see in them now?

Maybe she was making a fool of herself. Why would Cal want to make love to a woman he had every reason to dislike?

But then again, why wouldn't he?

The warm, clean shower spray rinsed their hair and sluiced down their bodies, running brown with African mud before it gurgled down the drain. A shiver of anticipation passed through Megan as Cal pushed her wet blouse off her shoulders. It slid down her arms and dropped to the tiles.

"Look at me, Megan." His voice was husky. His thumb caught the curve of her jaw, tilting her face upward. The eyes she'd remembered as cold burned with raw need.

Her hand moved upward to rest against his cheek. His

skin was warm, the stubble rough against her palm. "Kiss me, Cal," she whispered.

Leaning down, he feathered his lips against hers. The contact passed like a glowing thread of heat through her body, warming her to an aching awareness of how much she needed him. She strained upward to deepen the kiss and felt him respond, his arms pulling her close, his lips nibbling, tasting, moving to her cheeks, her throat and back to her mouth. His hand unhooked her bra and pushed at the waistband of her slacks. The fit was loose enough for them to slide off her hips and drop, along with her panties, to the shower floor. She stood naked in his arms—a trifle self-conscious because she was so thin, but Cal didn't seem to notice—or at least not to mind.

Finding a bar of scented soap, he lathered his hands and then reached for her, his palms slicking the warm suds across her shoulder blades and down the long furrow of her spine. Sweet sensations melted her body like hot fudge flowing over ice cream. Her tension eased out in a long sigh. Almost purring, she arched against the exquisite pressure of his hands. Her eyes closed as his fingers worked their delicious way down to trace the deep V of her lower back, splaying to cradle her buttocks. For a moment he held her that way, cupping her hips against his. Through his wet trousers she could feel the hard ridge of his sex pressing her belly.

A memory glimmered, awakening the cold coils that slumbered inside her. Megan willed herself to block the fear. She wanted to let Cal make love to her. She wanted to believe that she could heal. She wanted *him*.

He lowered his mouth to hers, his kiss gentle and lingering. "I want to touch all of you," he whispered, turning her around so that her back was toward him. His big soapy hands slid over her breasts, caressing them, cupping them in his palms, thumbing the nipples until they ached with yearning. A moan quivered in her throat.

"You're so beautiful, Megan. You were made to be loved." One hand lingered on her breast, and the other slid down to skim her navel, splay on her belly and brush the dark triangle of hair where her thighs joined. She wanted the burst of sensation that his touch would awaken when he explored further. But as his fingers moved lower, a chill passed through her body. The coils of fear shifted and tightened, and she sensed that she was losing the battle to hold them at bay.

Maybe things were happening too fast. If she took more time she might still be all right. Shifting away, she turned to face him.

"You need to clean up, too," she said, forcing a smile as she found the soap. "Let me wash your back."

Ignoring his slightly puzzled expression, she turned him away from her, pulled the mud-soaked shirt off his shoulders and tossed it onto the shower floor.

He had a magnificently sculpted back, broad and tanned and powerful. His smooth skin warmed to her touch. Megan luxuriated in the feel of him, letting her soapy hands glide over his muscular shoulders and down the solid, tapering curve of his spine. Little by little, as she stroked his warm, golden skin, she felt her fear ebbing. It was going to happen, she told herself. All she had to do was relax and let nature do the rest.

Reaching his waistband, she hesitated. With a raw laugh, Cal reached down, yanked open the fly and let his pants and briefs drop around his ankles. "Don't stop now," he said. "I'm enjoying this."

Ignoring a prickle of uneasiness, Megan soaped his taut buttocks. His body was perfect, everything tight and in flawless proportion. Any woman should be thrilled to have him in her bed. Her hands caressed curves and contours, moving forward to skim the ridges of his hip bones. She could feel the tension growing in him, sense the urgency in the harsh cadence of his breath. Her own pulse had begun to race—but was it from desire or from that unknown terror that had given her no peace since the night she'd gone after Saida?

He cleared his throat. "I think my back is clean enough. If you want to wash the rest of me, I'm all yours. Otherwise, just say so and I'll shut off the water and grab us some towels. I look forward to drying you off."

Megan glanced down at her soapy hands. Her heart lurched as she imagined Cal's jutting erection, gleaming like wet marble in her hands. She knew what he wanted. Heaven help her, she wanted it, too. But she could feel the cold dread, as sure and silent as death, rising inside her.

She froze.

"What is it, Megan?" He glanced back at her, his eyes narrowing with concern as he shut off the water. "What's the matter?"

She'd begun to shiver. Her arms clutched her ribs. Tears might have helped, but she hadn't shed them since that awful night in Darfur.

"I'm sorry." She choked out the words. "I thought I could do this, Cal. But I just can't. There's something wrong with me—something I can't control." She stared down at the shower drain, wishing she could just dissolve and flow away.

"You're getting cold." Stepping out onto the mat, he reached for one of the two white terry-cloth robes that hung on the back of the door. Gentleness masked his obvious frustration as he laid it over her trembling shoulders. Slipping her arms into the sleeves, she knotted the sash around her waist. Little by little her racing heart began to

A SINFUL SEDUCTION

calm. By the time she forced herself to look at him, he'd donned the other robe.

"I was hoping this wouldn't happen," she said. "I should've known better. I feel like a fool."

"At least I appreciate your honesty," he said. "I wouldn't want to make love to a woman who wasn't enjoying herself."

"Not even if she *wanted* to enjoy herself?" Megan gripped her sash, yanking it tighter around her waist. "Do you think I want to be this way—flying into a panic whenever I'm faced with intimacy? All I want is to be a normal woman again. So I took a chance. It didn't work. Not even with you."

Not even with you. It was too late to bite back the words. The subtle shift in his expression told her what he'd read into them. He wasn't just another man to her. He was a man who meant something—even if she wasn't completely sure what. Their past together had been so troubled, but the things she admired about him—his strength, his determination, the intensity of his feelings—had made her hope that he could carry some of this burden for her, lighten the load enough to let her heal.

"Come sit down." His hand at the small of her back guided her out of the bathroom and across the bedroom floor to the couch. Sitting, he pulled her down next to him and covered them both with a woolen blanket. Tucking her bare feet under her, she nestled into its warmth. Rain drummed on the tile roof and streamed down the windowpanes.

"You were amazing out there today," he said. "I mean it."

"It was an adventure—and somebody had to help."

He slipped an arm around her shoulders, a friendly gesture, meant to be comforting. "You're a brave woman,

Megan—and strong. I'm just discovering how strong. But something's frightened you badly. When did these panic attacks start?"

"Are you trying to analyze me, Dr. Freud?" She attempted a feeble joke.

"I'm just trying to understand you—maybe even help if I can. When did you become aware that something was wrong?"

"I'm not sure." She wasn't about to describe her fiasco with the doctor. That disastrous date wasn't the source of her problem, just a symptom.

"The incident you dreamed about—going after that young girl and boy, seeing them attacked. When was that?"

She shrugged, uneasy with the question. "Five, maybe six months ago. It's hard to keep track of time there. But I remember it was the dry season."

"Where were you when you saw it happen? If you were afraid to help them—"

"No, I was *trying* to help them. I'd brought a pistol. But before I could use it, somebody grabbed me from behind and took it away. I couldn't move, couldn't scream. I could only watch." Megan felt the fear rising. "Don't ask me to talk about this, Cal. I don't want to."

"Fine." His breath eased out in a long exhalation. "Just one more question. How did you get away?"

The cold coils tightened. "I don't know. Maybe the Janjaweed let me go because I was American. Or maybe somebody came from the camp and scared them off. The next thing I remember, I was waking up in the infirmary."

"You really don't know what happened?"

"I was probably knocked out—or fainted—and somebody found me. That's the only explanation that makes sense." Agitated now, she flung the blanket aside and rose from the couch. "No more questions, Cal. Two innocent young lives were destroyed that night. I'll remember it forever, but that doesn't mean I want to talk about it."

Pulse racing, she strode to the wardrobe where she'd hung her meager supply of clothes and went through the motions of rummaging through the hangers. "Isn't it about dinnertime? I'm starved, and I can hardly wear this bathrobe to the dining room. So please excuse me while I get dressed." She grabbed a set of clothes without really looking at them and glanced back at him. "That debacle in the shower never happened. I never want to hear about it again."

Cal glanced across the table to where Megan was conversing animatedly with Harris. Since he'd grilled her about the incident in the camp, she'd barely spoken to him. Clearly his questions had made her uncomfortable. All the more reason to keep pursuing them, but in a more subtle way.

He'd come to Tanzania to track down the stolen money and learn what he could about her role in Nick's suicide. That goal was still high on his list. But what drove him now was Megan—finding the key to understanding this maddeningly complex woman. He couldn't seem to make the pieces line up in his mind.

She had a fortune tucked away, but chose to work in one of the grimmest refugee camps in the world. She was equally at home in designer brands and mud-stained safari gear. She kissed him as if she couldn't get close enough to him, but froze at the feel of his hands on her body. She was brave but frightened. Passionate but withdrawn. Charming and at ease in this moment with Harris but still the same woman who had trembled with pain and fear barely an hour before.

The more he learned about her, the less he understood.

And the more driven he became to figure her out, find the key to unlock her inner demons and set her free.

Earlier he'd looked forward to making love to her. But even as she undressed him, he'd sensed that she was pushing herself too far. By the time she'd finally crumpled, he'd been prepared to back off. Bedding a terror-struck woman wasn't his idea of a good time—for him or for her.

Not even with you.

Her anguished words came back to him—the words that had told him he was more than just another man to her. She'd wanted him, and only him—the awareness of that made him all the more determined to break through her fear. Whatever it took, he would get to the bottom of what she was dealing with—and make love to her as she was meant to be loved.

A stray thought reminded him that he hadn't checked his email tonight. After dinner he would make his excuses and wander down the hall to the front desk. By now he should have a reply to his request for Megan's file. If it wasn't there, his next request would be less cordial.

By the time they'd finished their tiramisu, Cal was getting restless. It came as a relief when Megan accepted Harris's invitation to have a drink at the bar. Promising to join them later, he strode down the corridor to the front office. The computers were busy with people from the tour group using the antiquated machines, but he managed to find an empty spot and log on to his email.

The file was there, as he'd hoped. But it was a long one, and he didn't want to read it in this crowded room, with people jammed around him, awaiting their turn at the machines. Sending the file to the office printer, he picked up the sheaf of pages and went in search of some privacy.

Two doors down the hall from the dining room was a small library, the shelves stocked with books and out-of-date magazines left behind by past guests. It was furnished with two well-worn leather chairs, both empty. Switching on a lamp, Cal took a seat and began to read.

The first few pages were routine—lists of assignments and duties, along with evaluations, all of them praising her work. He was halfway through the file before he found what he was looking for—her medical history, including a doctor's account of the night Megan had described.

As he read, his fingers gripped the page, crumpling the edges of the paper.

Dear God. Megan...Megan...

Eight

With mounting horror, Cal reread the doctor's account—
how searchers had found Megan unconscious outside the
camp one morning, bruised and smeared with blood, her
clothes ripped away. She'd been eased onto a stretcher and
carried back to the infirmary, where an examination confirmed that she'd been raped, most likely multiple times.

For four days she'd lain in a stupor with an IV in her
arm. The medications she'd been given were listed in the
report—antibiotics along with a light sedative and drugs
to prevent pregnancy and sexually transmitted diseases.

The doctor had attempted to make arrangements to have
her airlifted to a hospital, but there was no plane readily
available. On the fifth day, while they were still awaiting
transport, Megan had opened her eyes and sat up. She'd
insisted that the flight be canceled and that she be allowed
to go back to work. She appeared to have made a full recovery except for one thing—when asked about the inci-

dent, she had no memory of anything beyond the attack on the young Sudanese girl.

Heartsick, Cal read the concluding paragraph.

After consulting with other medical staff, I made the decision that, given her emotionally fragile state, it would be a dangerous risk to inform Miss Cardston about the rape. It is my recommendation that she seek counseling at the first opportunity at which time she can be told and deal with the issue. Meanwhile, since she appears to be in good physical condition, and since we need her help, I see no reason why she shouldn't resume her work.

So Megan didn't know.

Cal sank back into the chair, feeling as if his blood had drained out his legs and onto the floor. No wonder she was scared at the thought of physical intimacy. No wonder she was having panic attacks. Her conscious mind had blocked the rape. But her body remembered and reacted with terror.

Lord, he'd done all the wrong things—grilling her with questions that made her feel vulnerable and under attack even when he wasn't touching her, pushing her to have sex with him, thinking he could fix her problems with a good old-fashioned roll in the sack. That Megan had been so willing to try, so desperate to feel normal again, made him feel like an even bigger heel.

The papers had slid off his lap and onto the floor. Cal gathered them up and folded them in half. He wasn't ready to go back to the bar and face Megan—especially in the presence of Harris and his teasing innuendos. And he needed to get the documents out of Megan's sight. It might be prudent to shred or burn them. But going back to them at a later time, when he'd had a chance to calm down, might give him more insight into her state of mind.

For now, he would take them back to the bungalow and hide them in his bag. Maybe the walk from the lodge would help clear his mind—as if anything could. He hadn't meant to get involved in Megan's problems. But he'd brought this mess on himself; and now he was in deep, way over his head.

"Another one?" Harris shot Megan a devilish grin as he signaled the waiter. "It's on Cal's bar tab, and he can bloody well afford it."

Megan shook her head. The man was shameless, but she couldn't help liking him. His outrageous manner, she sensed, hid a genuinely kind heart.

"One banana daiquiri's enough for me," she said. "Too much alcohol gives me a headache. Maybe you should think about cutting back yourself. All that whiskey can't be good for you."

He lifted his freshly refilled glass. The cut crystal reflected glints of flame from the candle on their table. "No lectures, m'dear. An old man like me has few enough pleasures in life—a sunrise over the Serengeti…an occasional drink with a pretty lass…and the taste of a good Scotch on your client's dime. Doesn't quite make up for coming home to an empty bed, but it's close enough." He sipped from the glass, taking time to savor the taste. "Speaking of beds, how are you and Cal getting along in that cozy bungalow?"

Megan felt the heat creep up to the roots of her hair, embarrassed not just by the indelicate question but by the memory of how close they'd come to being *very* cozy— before her panic ruined things. "All right. We've made some…accommodations."

"Right sorry about the mix-up," he said. "When Cal told me he was bringing a lady friend along, I just assumed…"

"You assumed wrong. But it was an honest mistake."

"When I saw that kiss today, I was hoping it wasn't a mistake, after all."

Megan faked a chuckle. "We were just celebrating our safe getaway. Nothing's changed."

"I'll just have to take your word for that, won't I?" He gave her a knowing look. What would he do if he knew the truth? Would he offer her fatherly advice or just shake his head in disbelief? "Speaking of Cal, where do you suppose the lad's run off to? I'm beginning to wonder if he's lost his taste for my company."

"He said something about checking his email." Feeling the need for a break, Megan rose. "Why don't I go and look for him? I shouldn't be long."

Harris rose with her, minding his manners. "I'll be right here. If you don't come back, I'll assume you've found another diversion." The teasing light in his eye gave way to something warmer and more genuine. "Whatever's happening between you two, I can tell he cares for you. Whenever you step into view, you're all that he sees."

Don't. Megan bit back the word. Harris was pulling her strings; that was all. The old man enjoyed stirring up intrigue.

"Take your umbrella with you," he said. "You may want to go outside."

With a murmur of thanks, Megan took the umbrella Cal had left with her and walked down the hall to the front desk. Cal wasn't in the computer alcove, but the clerk told her he'd been there and had printed out a file before leaving.

Glancing around the lodge, she failed to find him. Why hadn't he joined her and Harris in the bar? Had he received some unsettling news? Would she find him in the bungalow packing his bag to leave?

Cal was a busy man, she reminded herself. He had

responsibilities and concerns in the outside world. If he needed to fly home, she'd be a fool to take it personally, or to expect any kind of promise to return. But she would always wonder what might have happened between them if he'd stayed. Would they have found some answers to whatever they were seeking—or only more disappointment?

Megan opened the umbrella and stepped outside to find that the rain had stopped. The clouds had moved on, leaving a glorious panoply of stars in a sky as black as a panther's coat. Closing the umbrella, she hurried down the brick path. Cal was an adult, she reminded herself. There was no need to go looking for him. But a sixth sense whispered that something had changed—something that had stopped him from rejoining her and Harris. She needed to find out what it was.

Cal had hidden the volunteer report between the folds of the map, which he'd zipped into the inner pocket of his duffel. Now, seated on the bench under the window, he pondered what to do next.

Sharing what he'd learned with Megan was out of the question. He was sure that her first reaction, if she learned what he'd done, would be fury at him for accessing her private information. But that much he could live with. It was the reaction that would follow, once she discovered the information in the file itself, that had him more worried. How would it affect her to know she'd been raped?

Would the awareness push her over the edge—or might it be cathartic, even helpful? Either way, he couldn't be the one to tell her. He had no right to make that decision—nor did he want to. He agreed with the doctor who'd written the report. Megan would need professional help to deal with the way she'd been hurt. And here in the wilds of Africa, there was little help of that kind to be had.

So what now? Should he try to get her back to the States? He couldn't imagine she'd be willing to go without knowing why. Should he try to help her himself, maybe get her talking? Lord, he wouldn't know where to begin. In his blundering way, he could make things worse.

For now, he could only behave as if nothing had changed. Megan was a proud woman and she was smart. If he showed pity or an excess of concern toward her, she'd pick up on it. And she'd demand to know what was wrong.

Leaning back on the bench, he closed his eyes and let the memories of the day crumble around him. Warring emotions flailed at him from all sides—worry, rage and frustration. He found himself wishing he could find a wall and punch it till his knuckles bled.

Megan hadn't asked him to come and find her, Cal reminded himself. She hadn't asked him to get involved in her life. But he *was* involved, and now he couldn't just walk away.

For the first time he found himself asking whether Megan had suffered enough. Whether she was guilty or innocent in the embezzlement, surely she'd paid the price for anything she might have done. If she returned to the States, there'd be legal entanglements—the civil suit he'd filed against her after she'd disappeared had been the first and not the last—but he could withdraw his own charges and hire a lawyer to help her with the rest.

But what was he thinking? The money was missing and his best friend was dead. How could he let that go without learning more about what had happened? He still needed answers, still had to understand what kind of person Megan truly was. The report was just the tip of the iceberg. There was still so much he wanted to know.

"Cal?" Her low voice startled him out of his reverie. "What are you doing out here? Is everything all right?"

"Fine," he lied. "I must've dozed off."

"Why didn't you come back to the bar? Harris was concerned about you."

"Sorry. The rain had stopped. I felt like some fresh air. I'll apologize to Harris tomorrow." More lies. Megan deserved better. But if he was going to be around her, lies were something he'd have to get used to.

Coming around the bench, she stood gazing down at him. She looked so fresh and pretty with the stars behind her and the night mist glistening on her hair. *Brave, sweet Megan...how could those bastards have hurt you the way they did?*

"You're sure everything's all right?" she asked. "The desk clerk mentioned you'd printed a file."

"Just business. Something that needed my okay." Another lie.

"When you didn't come back, I was afraid I'd find you packing your bags."

"I wouldn't do that without telling you." That much, at least, was true. "Sit down. It's a nice night, and it's too early to go in."

She took a seat on the bench, at a stranger's distance. Cal guessed she was still smarting from their near miss in the shower. He ached to cradle her in his arms, but he pushed the urge away, struggling to rebuild the emotional walls that had always kept him strong and centered, thinking clearly. They'd taken a bad blow tonight, and he felt uncomfortably certain that Megan's warm body in his arms would wreck them completely. He had to stay focused and rational, and not lose sight of why he was here.

"Was Harris upset about being abandoned in the bar?" he asked, making small talk.

"I hope not. He told me that as long as the drinks were on your tab, he'd be fine." She shifted her gaze to the stars. "I get the feeling Harris is a better man than he pretends to be."

"You're right. He'd deny it if you asked, but I know for a fact he's paying to educate Gideon's children. And no one works harder to make sure his clients are safe and taken care of. I'd trust the old man with my life—and have."

She gave him a tentative smile. "Somehow that doesn't surprise me. What's the real story behind his losing that arm?"

"I haven't a clue, and I've heard at least a dozen different versions. Part of his white hunter mystique, I suspect. Harris is one of a dying breed. These days, your safari guide is more likely to be African."

"That's as it should be, I suppose. Still, there's that old Hollywood image—John Wayne, Clark Gable…" A visible shiver passed through her body. She'd worn a light jacket to dinner but now the night air was getting chilly.

"Stay put. I'll get a blanket." Rising, Cal strode inside. Tonight Megan seemed relaxed and willing to talk. He very much wanted her to stay that way.

Seconds later he returned with the blanket. She snuggled into one end, leaving the rest for him.

"Better?" Cal pulled his end of the blanket over his chest.

"Better, thanks. The sky's beautiful tonight, isn't it?"

Cal murmured his agreement, suppressing the urge to circle her shoulders with his arm and pull her close.

"I always wanted Nick to take me with him to Africa when he made trips for the foundation. But when I asked him, he told me I wouldn't like it. Can you imagine that?"

"Imagine your not liking it?" Cal shook his head. "Not after seeing you out there today." Back in California, he might have agreed with Nick that his pampered, high-maintenance wife was ill-suited to the wilderness. He knew better now…and suddenly found himself wondering just how well Nick had bothered to get to know his wife.

Her smile flickered in the darkness. "Oh, today was wonderful. But it's not just the wild country and the animals I love. It's the people—like those poor souls in Darfur. They've suffered unthinkable wrongs, lost their homes and their loved ones, seen their women raped and their young boys marched off to be soldiers. But I see so much courage in the camps, so much selflessness—the way they take care of each other and share what little they have. They're the reason I want to go back to that awful place, Cal. The reason I *need* to go back."

Gazing at her, he shook his head. After what had happened to her, how could she even think of going back to Darfur?

"You're quite a woman, Megan." The understatement was deliberate. To say more might reveal too much.

"It's not me. It's them. They showed me the person I was meant to be—the person I'm still trying to become. I know that might sound maudlin to a man like you, but it's the truth."

"A man like me?" Cal quirked an eyebrow, teasing her a little to lighten the mood. "How am I supposed to take that?"

"Oh, not badly, I hope. But you've always struck me as a very pragmatic man, more focused on charging ahead and getting things done than on sentiment."

"A cold-blooded cynic, in other words."

"I didn't say that." Something flashed in her eyes. She looked away, her gaze tracing the path of a falling star. She used to do that back in California—find some excuse to turn away from him whenever they talked. What had she been hiding? Dissatisfaction with her glittering lifestyle? Unhappiness in her personal life? Or…had she been hiding something more sinister, such as her crimes against the organization where she now worked?

As he studied her sharply etched profile, a thread of doubt crept into his mind. Had Megan really changed? Could he take her words at face value, or was she conning him? What if the money was still out there, waiting to be drawn on when she felt safe enough—or when she'd volunteered long enough to salve her guilty conscience?

The report verified everything she'd told him, Cal reminded himself. Her spotless service record was real. The rape was real. But so was the crime that had come before all of that. Someone was responsible for taking the money, and Cal still didn't want to believe it was the friend he would have entrusted with his life.

He didn't realize how long they'd been silent until she spoke.

"Looking back, I don't think Nick knew me at all— maybe because I didn't know myself. I became what I thought he wanted. Not that it made any difference in the end."

Cal shot her a startled glance. Her words matched his own thoughts, but he was surprised to hear her bring it up. She'd seemed firmly against discussing Nick with him earlier. "I thought you and Nick had the perfect marriage," he prompted, testing the waters. "It certainly looked that way."

She gazed up at the sky. "We put on a good show. But we both knew better."

"Would you have stayed with him?"

"You mean, if he hadn't shot himself when the money scandal broke? I've asked myself the same question. I was raised to believe that marriage vows are sacred. But when your partner is cheating and doesn't care how much he hurts you, those vows can seem more like a prison sentence. Maybe if I hadn't lost the baby…" Her voice trailed off.

So Nick had been cheating on her. The discovery tightened a raw knot in the pit of Cal's stomach. He and Nick had been best friends since high school. True blue all the way, or so he'd thought. But if Nick had been faithless to his beautiful wife, what else would he have been capable of?

"What happened with the baby, Megan?" he asked. "Nick never said much, except that you'd lost it."

"That doesn't surprise me. I'd hoped having a baby might make a difference, force him to take our marriage more seriously, but it barely seemed to register with him. As for the miscarriage…" She shrugged. "It was what it was—nothing I could have prevented. At least that's what the doctor said. I've always wanted children. But maybe it isn't in the cards. Especially not now."

Cal studied her profile in the faint light. How could any man have cheated on a woman like Megan? Nick had always been a flirt, quick with compliments and flattery whenever a beautiful woman was involved, even after he was married. Cal had simply chalked it up as part of his friend's personality. He'd never imagined the man would cheat—Nick had given every indication of worshipping his beautiful wife. Had it really all been for show?

There was no denying the aching resignation in Megan's tone. Nick hadn't just indulged in an indiscretion or two—it sounded as if Megan was saying he'd never been faithful at all. Now that Cal thought about it, Nick had always been one to take his commitments lightly. Instead of apologizing for missed meetings or deadlines, he was more likely to brush it off with a shrug and a smile, confident that he could charm his way into forgiveness. The truth of that hurt like hell. But how much more had it hurt Megan?

If things were different between them, Cal thought, he might try to make it up to her—show her how a woman should be treated by a man who claimed to care for her.

But given the past, that wasn't in the cards, either.

Megan wrapped the blanket tighter, taking care to leave enough slack for Cal. The moon had risen above the distant hills. Full and ripe as an August peach from her grandmother's old tree, it flooded the brick terrace with light and etched Cal's craggy face into ridges and shadows. She'd thought she'd managed to put her old life behind her. But being with Cal had brought it all back—and not in a good way.

"Maybe the camps have been an outlet for your mothering instincts," he said.

"Are you trying to analyze me again?" She didn't like being examined, especially by Cal.

"I wouldn't dream of it," he said. "But as long as we're on the subject, wouldn't it be worth getting professional help for those panic attacks and nightmares?"

"Maybe." A prickle of distrust stirred. She faked a chuckle. "If I could find a good witch doctor to rattle the bones."

"You're not going to find help here." He turned on the bench, impaling her with his eyes. "I've glimpsed the pain you're in, Megan. Come home with me and get the therapy you need. I'll do whatever it takes to help you."

Megan lowered her gaze, alarms going off in her head. Of course, she told herself. This was why Cal had come here. He was determined to get her back to the States, where he could go after her legally, maybe even have her arrested. This wasn't the approach she'd expected him to take, but the end result was the same either way.

And she'd actually begun to trust him. What a fool she'd been!

Meeting his eyes again, she shook her head. "Cal, I know you mean well." *A necessary lie.* "But I'm not leaving Africa. If I were to go home, there's a chance I'd never make it back here."

"Not even if I promised to send you?"

"I can't depend on that. Things get in the way. Besides, there's nothing wrong with me that time and hard work won't heal."

"But to go back to the very place where—" He broke off, as if he'd been about to say too much.

"Don't you see? That's exactly what I need to do—go back and deal with what happened. If I can face it, and understand it, it won't have the power to frighten me."

The breath exploded out of him. "Damn it, Megan, if you'd just listen—"

"Stop pushing me, Cal. I'm not a child."

"You're working for my organization. I can order you home for treatment."

"Not if I resign. Believe me, there are plenty of NGOs who'd be happy to have an experienced nurse." She stood, tossing the blanket aside. "I'm too tired to argue any more. If you'll excuse me, I'm going to turn in. Truce, all right?"

"Truce." He rose with a weary sigh. "I'll go and spend some time with Harris. That'll give you a chance to get settled. We'll be off to another early start tomorrow."

"Fine." She opened the door, which was unlocked.

"Megan."

She turned at the sound of her name.

"Take your side of the bed. I promise to be a perfect gentleman."

A gentleman? Is that what he called someone who flew halfway around the world to hound a woman into his idea

of justice? Did he really think she didn't know about the
civil suits waiting to fall on her the minute she reentered
the United States? What kind of gentleman—what kind of
man—was he to do this to her and pretend it was for her
own good? She was angry with herself for even listening
to him, much less beginning to trust him. And that wasn't
even mentioning the way she'd let him kiss her, or the way
she'd started to feel in the shower with him before her fear
had taken over. For a short while, she'd actually thought
that he was the man who could make things better for her.

She stepped into the bungalow and closed the door. If
only she could close the door as easily on her frustrating
feelings toward the man.

Nine

By the time Cal crossed the grounds to the bungalow, the moon had risen above the treetops. A bat flashed past his head, its wings slicing the dark like scimitars. The haunting cry of an owl shimmered through the night.

He'd spent the better part of two hours with Harris, gently urging him to call it a night and go to bed. The old hunter hadn't looked well tonight—not really sick, but sad and fatigued. At sixty-six, his rough life and hard drinking had begun to catch up with him, and it showed. Cal had been worried enough to stay with him and walk him to his private room in the rear of the lodge. It would be a relief to get him away from this place and out on the Serengeti with no hotel bar to keep him up drinking at night.

The bungalow was dark. Hopefully Megan would be asleep. She'd been tired, too—and prickly, he recalled. He should have known better than to bring up the idea of flying her home for therapy. But she'd given him an opening. He'd seized it and come away with his whiskers singed.

He'd learned where she stood on the question of going home. But he also knew something Megan didn't. She needed serious help—and going back to Darfur without that help could send her spiraling into an emotional abyss.

Unlocking the door, he stepped inside. Moonlight fell between the parted curtains, softening the darkness. Relief lifted his mood as he glanced through the mosquito netting and saw the slight form raising the covers. At least she'd trusted him enough to share the bed. Or maybe she'd wanted him close by to protect her from the lurking monsters in her dreams.

Moving closer, he gazed down at her. She lay curled with her lovely rump toward his side of the bed, sleeping as sweetly as a child. Something tightened around Cal's heart. Whatever phantoms threatened that innocent slumber, he wanted to be there to drive them away. He understood himself, and he knew these protective feelings toward her might not last for long, not when he still had so many questions and doubts. But while Megan was suffering, he couldn't turn his back and walk away from her.

He undressed in the dark. Clad in his skivvies and undershirt, he walked around the bed. He slept raw at home and had planned to do the same on this trip. If he'd foreseen that he'd be sharing a room—and a bed—with a woman he'd resolved to treat like a kid sister, he'd have brought along some pajamas.

He did have a pack of condoms in his bag, which he'd bought at the hotel gift shop in Arusha after making plans to take Megan on safari—and hopefully seduce her. But they were locally made, so he couldn't count on their reliability. Given the present arrangement, maybe that was just as well.

Doing his best not to wake her, he lifted the blanket and slid over the top sheet onto his side of the bed. The mattress wasn't king-size, or even queen-size. It was a double, like the one his grandparents had slept on all their married life. There was no boundary line down the middle, but Megan was definitely taking more than her share of space. Unless he wanted to sleep on the couch, he would have to choose between disturbing her rest to move her over or spooning around her. The latter struck him as the more appealing choice.

Easing deeper into the bed, he curved his body around hers and pulled the blankets up to his shoulders. Head on the pillow, he closed his eyes. It was late, and he was tired. With any luck he'd go right to sleep.

But something told him it wasn't going to be that easy. Megan's warmth crept around him, seeping into his senses. She smelled of the lavender soap from the shower. It was the same soap he'd used, but on her woman's skin the innocent aroma, coupled with the memory of that shower, was sensual enough to rock his libido. The notion that he mustn't touch her, mustn't have her, heated his blood like torched gasoline. He bit back a groan as his sex rose and hardened. Only the thin sheet between their bodies kept his male impulses in check.

It was going to be a long night.

Megan stirred and opened her eyes. Except for a shaft of moonlight falling through the window, the room was dark. She'd gone to bed alone. But the sound of breathing and the manly warmth radiating against her back told her she was alone no longer. Sometime in the night Cal had joined her.

As she drifted into wakefulness, she became aware of her curled position in the bed. Moving in her sleep, she'd left Cal with little more than the far edge of the mattress.

Instead of pushing her out of the way, she realized, he'd done his best to sleep around her.

Despite the awkwardness between them, she would have to give him credit for being a gentleman in this respect, at least. True to his word, he hadn't laid a hand on her. But he'd stayed close, and even in her sleep, something about his presence had made her feel safe and peaceful. Maybe that was why the dreams hadn't come tonight.

Stretching full length, she rolled toward her own side of the mattress. Looking back, she could see Cal. He lay awake with one arm propping his head. Had he been watching over her?

"Hello," she whispered. "Did I wake you?"

He shook his head. "Any bad dreams?"

"No. But I don't always have them. When did you come in?"

"A couple of hours ago. You were sleeping like a kitten."

"All over the bed! No wonder you're still awake. You should've booted me back where I belong."

His chuckle warmed her. "You looked so contented, I didn't have the heart."

"There's plenty of room for you now," she said. "Go ahead and stretch out. I won't bite you."

"I won't touch that comment." The bed creaked slightly as he eased onto his back and straightened his legs. "Ah… that's better," he breathed.

"Now get some sleep," she ordered. "And don't let me crowd you again."

Another chuckle was followed by silence, as if he'd bitten back a too-clever retort.

They lay side by side, modestly clad and separated by a thin layer of muslin sheet that might as well have been a brick wall. There was something Victorian about the arrangement, like two strangers sharing a bed in a nineteenth-century inn. Megan knew that Cal had come up with this silliness to ease her fear. But no barrier could hide the intense masculinity exuded by the man next to her.

Even when she was married to Nick, Cal's presence had given her a rush of heightened awareness. She'd willed herself to ignore the sensation, but he was so powerful, so decisive and rugged that he fluttered the pulse of every female who came within range. Next to him, even the glib and charming Nick had seemed shallow and insubstantial. Cal was like the lion they'd seen in the crater—fierce, majestic and completely sure of himself. She'd be foolish to trust him—he was every bit as dangerous as the lion. But she couldn't deny her attraction to him.

Cal had never had any shortage of women. And he was doubtless an accomplished lover. She remembered the touch of his big hands in the shower, how he'd caressed her naked breasts until she'd ached for more. He'd awakened feelings she thought she'd lost forever. She'd *wanted* him—and she'd desperately needed the release he could give her.

So why had she stopped him? What gave her fear such uncontrollable power? If only she could understand that much, she might be on her way to healing.

"Are you all right, Megan?" His throaty whisper stirred the darkness.

"Aren't you supposed to be asleep?"

"Aren't you?" He paused, then turned toward her, shifting onto his side. "Feel like talking?"

Talking? Megan could guess what that meant. He was preparing to back her into a corner and grill her again, maybe about Nick and the money, or about her time in Darfur, or even what had happened in the shower that afternoon. Why did *she* always have to be the one answering questions?

"I've done enough talking," she said. "I'd rather listen for a change. Tell me about yourself."

"Not much to tell. My story's pretty dull compared with yours. Nick must've told you most of it."

"Not really. Just that the two of you were friends in high school and decided to start J-COR after college. But I don't want to talk about Nick. Where did you grow up?"

"Fresno. White house. Picket fence. Barbecue in the backyard. Station wagon in the driveway. How does it sound so far? Are you getting sleepy?"

"Don't count on it." She shifted deeper under the covers, her hip brushing his through the sheet. The contact triggered a subtle ache—a yearning to snuggle against his side and lie cloaked in his warmth. She battled temptation, telling herself that any move on her part would only confuse the man, leading him to assume she wanted more.

Maybe she *did* want more. But a second failure on her part would be frustrating for him and scathingly humiliating for her. Better to leave well enough alone. She sighed, willing herself to remain where she lay. "Go on," she urged him. "I'm listening."

Cal's words could have painted a pretty picture of his childhood home. It would have been a true picture, as far as the description went. But that would mean leaving out the screaming, cursing fights that raged between his parents within the walls of that home. Those fights had driven him out of the house to wander the streets at all hours, afraid of what he'd see if he came back too soon.

Sharing that part of his life was painful. But Megan had been open with him about her past. He owed her as much.

"My mother left us when I was eleven," he said. "My father made sure I knew she'd run off with another man—

one who'd told her he didn't want a snot-nosed kid like me tagging along."

"You were an only child?"

"Yes, fortunately."

"And your mother never came back?"

"We got word years later that she'd died of cancer. By then I was in high school. I can't say I blamed her for leaving—my dad was pretty rough on her, and it may have been her only way out. But the fact that she didn't even tell me goodbye or write me a letter…that part was hard to take."

"Oh, Cal…"

His jaw tightened. If there was one thing he couldn't stand it was pity from a woman—especially *this* woman.

"No need to be sorry," he said, cutting her off before she could shovel on more sympathy. "I got through it fine. My dad sold cars and hung out with his drinking buddies. I took after-school jobs—mowing lawns, bagging groceries, lifeguarding at the pool. The work kept me in spending money and out of trouble. I earned my own car, bought my own clothes and still managed to do pretty well in school. Even dated a few girls and played a little football."

"And that was when you met Nick."

"Yeah. You know the rest." They'd shared a table in study hall and, for some reason he couldn't even remember, they'd hit it off. The big, scrappy kid from the wrong side of town and the handsome, smooth-talking boy who seemed to have everything—two doting parents, an imposing brick home and a black Trans Am to drive to school. They'd formed an alliance that had lasted until two years ago, when a single gunshot had ended it all.

Remembering that part still hurt like hell.

Megan stirred beside him, warm and soft and fragrant. "I know you cared about him, Cal," she said. "I cared about him, too. Nick had some wonderful qualities. But he hurt us both. I've done my best to forgive him and move on. I hope you have, too."

Cal's throat went painfully tight. He had no words—and even if he had, he wouldn't have been able to speak. All he could do was hook her with his arm and draw her close while raw emotions surged through his body. It wasn't a lustful gesture, just one of simple human need, and she seemed to know it. Her head settled into the hollow of his shoulder. Her breath eased as she fitted her body to his side. It felt good holding her like this, even with nothing else in the plan. Little by little he could feel the tension flowing out of him.

Turning his head, he brushed a kiss across her hairline. "Go to sleep, Megan," he whispered.

She didn't reply, but her nearness said enough. Lord, but she was sweet. Almost sweet enough to make him forget their shared past. But some wrongs were too grievous to put aside. For him, there could be no forgiving and no moving on until he knew the full story behind Nick's death, the stolen money and Megan's part in it all.

Megan lay still, lulled by the steady beat of Cal's heart. His skin was warm through the thin fabric of his undershirt. She closed her eyes, feeling the gentle rise and fall of his chest against her cheek.

Tonight he'd shared some surprising secrets—things that not even Nick had told her about his friend. Surely Nick had known Cal's background; but maybe he hadn't expected her to be interested. Sadly, now that she thought of it, there were a lot of things she and Nick hadn't talked about.

She tried to picture Cal as a lonely, unwanted young boy, abandoned by his mother and probably ignored by his father. No wonder he'd developed a cold manner and a cynical attitude. No wonder he'd never trusted any woman enough to develop a serious relationship.

The only person Cal seemed to have trusted was Nick. And in the end, even Nick had betrayed him. His anguish would have been as deep as her own—different, yes, but just as painful and just as lasting.

Cal's revelation gave her new understanding and an unexpected sense of peace—like a gift. She wasn't alone in her pain. In his own way, Cal was suffering, too; and he was looking for answers. Why else would he have come all this way to find her?

She was beginning to drift. Most nights she dreaded sleep and the nightmares it brought. But tonight she felt safe. Cal was here to protect her and calm her fears. For now that was enough.

Was she getting better?

But it was too soon to ask that question. The past three days had been intoxicatingly normal, with drives into the crater and along the river where the elephants came to drink. They'd seen crocodiles, great, lumbering hippos and more lions, a pride of them with cubs. They'd scouted a tree where a leopard had hung its kill and, after some searching, managed to spot the beautiful, mottled cat sprawled along a high limb.

Megan had filled her camera's memory card with photos and her head with stunning images that would stay with her the rest of her life. But did that really mean she was getting better?

She felt vital and restored; and the nightmares had yet to return. But it wasn't as if she could spend the rest of her life on safari. How would she hold up in the world she'd left behind—especially in Darfur?

As for Cal, they'd managed a cautious truce. He treated her like a friend and kept his distance both in and out of bed. If it wasn't everything she wanted—and there were times when she ached for more—at least she felt safe with him.

His touch on her arm tugged her back to the present. They were driving the crater today, on the narrow track where they'd been mired in the rain. Gideon had slowed the Land Rover to a crawl. A hundred yards ahead, a hulking dark shape moved through a screen of thornbush. Cal's lips moved, forming the words *black rhino*.

They'd cut the distance by half when the rhino burst out of the bush, coming straight toward them. The beast was immense—not tall like an elephant, but massive—long-bodied and as sleekly powerful as an old-time steam locomotive. The horn on its nose was as long as Megan's arm and looked to be spindle-sharp at the tip.

Megan forgot to breathe as the rhino paused, ears and nostrils twitching. Her hand crept into Cal's as Gideon idled the engine. They were close—too close. Rhinos were known to be short-tempered, and this one was capable of wrecking the vehicle and trampling or tossing anyone who couldn't get away. Harris had drawn and cocked the rifle—not to shoot the precious beast but more likely to try to scare it if the need arose.

The rhino snorted and tossed its enormous head. The small brown birds roosting on its back flapped upward, chattering an alarm—not a good sign.

At a touch from Harris, Gideon eased the Land Rover into Reverse and began slowly backing away. A bead of sweat trickled down the side of the driver's face. No one in the vehicle moved or spoke as the wheels inched backward.

Snorting again, the rhino lowered its head. Sunlight glinted on the deadly black horn. Megan's grip tightened around Cal's hand. His body tensed, moving slightly in front of her.

But the rhino must have calculated that the intruders weren't worth bothering with. Changing course, the huge beast turned aside and trotted into the scrub. Gideon gunned the vehicle backward, stopping only once they were safely out of range. Pulling the hand brake, he sagged over the wheel. Harris uncocked the rifle, breaking the silence with a laugh. "Well, hell, I said I wanted to show you a black rhino, didn't I?"

"That you did." Cal's arm went around Megan's shoulders, squeezing her fiercely tight. Megan managed a nervous chuckle.

"I don't suppose I can talk you into going back, can I?" she joked. "I forgot to take pictures."

Still giddy from the rush of their close call, they headed out of the crater. Sullen clouds were rumbling over the rim, and nobody wanted to be caught in the rain again. Tomorrow they'd be leaving Ngorongoro for a tent camp on the vast Serengeti grassland to the north. What remained of the afternoon would be set aside for resting, washing and packing up for a predawn start.

By dinnertime Megan had her things well organized. She'd enjoyed the lodge but she was ready for a change of scene. Over plates of coq au vin and rice pilaf, Harris described what she could expect to see.

"We'll be there for the big game migration that happens every year with the rains. Nothing like it on earth. Wildebeest, zebra and more—oceans of them—marching south to new grass. Bloody picnic for the meat-eaters that tag along. Not a pretty sight for a lady, but I shouldn't worry about you. After all, you've been in Darfur."

Cal glanced toward her. She caught the dark flicker in his eyes before he looked away. Was he thinking about the nightmares and panic attacks she'd come on safari to escape—details he'd agreed not to share with Harris? Was he worried about how she'd react to the more violent aspects of the migration?

It would be like Cal to worry. That was one thing Megan had learned about him on this outing—that he paid attention to everyone around him and seemed to feel responsible for their well-being. That included her—sometimes to her annoyance.

They finished their dessert. Then, as had become custom, Megan rose, excused herself and went back to the bungalow to shower and relax while Cal stayed to keep Harris company. Not only did the arrangement give her some needed private time, but it helped ensure that Harris would make it back to his room without drinking too much. Cal had voiced his concern for the old hunter, and Megan had agreed that Harris shouldn't be left alone at night in the bar.

After showering and dressing in her pajamas and robe, she curled up on the couch with the afghan and a paperback murder mystery she'd borrowed from the lodge's library. The book had looked promising, but the story wasn't holding her attention. She'd already guessed how it would end, and a peek at the last page proved her right.

Setting the book on the coffee table, she leaned back into the cushions and tried to imagine what the next few days would be like. She knew about the migration and had even seen video footage of it on PBS's *Nature*. But being there, actually seeing it, would be a thrill to remember.

The more she thought about it, the more she wished she'd asked Harris more questions. How soon would they get to the Serengeti? What would they see on the way?

Maybe it would help to look at a map. Cal had a map,

she remembered now. He'd mentioned that he kept it in his bag.

Crossing the room, she found the packed duffel where he'd left it on the floor of the wardrobe. Her fingers probed inside and felt the stiffness of paper in the inner pocket. Unzipping the pocket, she lifted out the folded map, which felt thicker than she'd expected.

As she unfolded the map, a sheaf of printed papers dropped out and scattered on the tiles. Bending to gather them up, Megan noticed a name at the top of one page.

Her name.

Ten

Roiling clouds blackened the night sky, hiding the moon and stars. Lightning sheeted across the horizon, followed seconds later by the subtle roar of distant thunder. Walking the brick path back to the bungalow, Cal was grateful that Harris had decided to turn in early. Otherwise he'd be running a gauntlet through the coming downpour.

As it was, he took his time. Today, under the equatorial sun, the humid air had felt like a thick flannel blanket. Tonight the breeze was cool, the air sweet in his lungs. The day had been a good one, crowned by the close brush with the rare black rhino. When Megan's hand had crept into his, he'd felt the connection of electric fear and excitement that coursed through both their bodies. In that breathless moment when the beast was threatening to charge, his foremost thought had been keeping her safe.

Was he falling for the woman? But that would be the craziest thing he could do. Megan was an emotional wreck.

And whether she did or didn't have anything to do with the stolen money, their past history didn't bode well for any kind of relationship.

But things weren't that simple. As attracted as he'd been to her beauty, he was even more drawn to her now that he'd seen her courage, her kindness and her magnificent spirit. Lying next to her in the night, separated by nothing but that damnable sheet, he'd burned with wanting her. It had been all he could do to keep from ripping away the thin muslin, seizing her in his arms and burying his swollen sex in that deep, hot wetness he craved like a drowning man craves air.

But that would be the most despicable—and damaging—thing he could do.

Reaching the porch of the bungalow, he fished for his key. The curtain was drawn, but the glow of a single lamp shone through the fabric. Would he find her awake, maybe reading that paperback she'd found in the lodge? That might not be so bad, he mused. This would be their last night in the bungalow—maybe their last chance for some relaxing, private talk.

After a polite knock to announce his presence, he turned the key and opened the door.

Megan was seated on the couch, wrapped in the afghan. Her back was ramrod straight, her fists clenched in her lap. The rigid expression on her face made it clear that something terrible had happened. Cal's heart dropped as he saw the papers laid out on the coffee table.

He stifled a groan. "Megan—"

Her look stopped him from saying more—raw eyes, filled with shock and a kind of frozen rage.

"How long have you known?" Her hoarse whisper rose from a well of pain.

Cal forced his mouth to form words. "Not long. A few

days. I can imagine what you think, but I was looking for a way to help you."

"Help me?" She flung the words at him. "By going behind my back? This was private information. You had no right!"

"That's where you're wrong. As the head of the foundation, I have the right to see volunteer records."

She glared at him in helpless fury. Cal stood his ground, hoping that a cool facade might help keep her calm. But he didn't feel cool. Heaven help him, what had he done to this woman?

"So why didn't you tell me?" Megan was beginning to crumble. "How long did you plan to keep it to yourself that I'd been...*raped?*" She choked on the last word.

Cal ached to gather her into his arms. But he knew better than to try. She was too angry to welcome comfort, especially from him. "You saw the report," he said. "The doctor didn't think you were ready to be told. Not without professional help."

"The doctor was *wrong!*" She was on her feet, eyes blazing. "He was wrong, and so were you! I'm not a child! I *needed* to know! How could I heal without understanding what happened to me?"

"I'm sorry. I deferred to the doctor's judgment. I didn't feel I had the background to make any other call." Lord, he sounded so detached. She probably thought he was the world's coldest bastard.

"You should have told me, anyway." The afghan had slipped off her shoulders. She let it fall to the floor. "It would have been a kindness to tell me, Cal. Instead, you let me make a fool of myself. That time in the shower— did you know then?"

"No. If I had, things would never have gone that far."

He took another step toward her. "Sit down, and talk to me, Megan."

"Why should I? You went behind my back. You kept a secret from me—a terrible secret—"

Her fists came up to flail impotently at his chest. He stood like a pillar, letting the harmless blows glance off him. He deserved her anger for the way he'd let her down. The last thing he'd wanted to do was to hurt her again—and yet, that was exactly what he'd done.

As her strength ebbed, she began to quiver. Her shoulders slumped. She buried her face in her palms. Sobs shook her thin frame. Cal had always prided himself on his ability to manage a crisis. But trying to reason with Megan had only made things worse. Now he had run out of things to say. There was only one thing left to do.

Without another word, he wrapped her in his arms and held her tight.

Outside, the storm had broken. Lightning crashed across the sky, flickering through the curtains as the thunder roared overhead. Rain battered the windowpanes and drummed on the roof, like an echo of the emotions that churned through Megan's body.

Pressed against Cal, she had no will to pull away. She was still furious, but she needed the solid anchor of his strength. Tonight, as she'd waited for him to come back from the lodge, she'd struggled to remember what had happened on that tragic night. The details of the brutal assault on Saida had haunted her dreams for months. But she had no recollection of the same thing happening to her.

Had she been unconscious at the time, or had her mind mercifully blocked the memory? And what of the physical signs of assault? She supposed that thanks to the swift treatment she received, and the four days she spent in a daze, the worst of the injuries had time to heal before she came back to full awareness. If only the mental and emotional damage were as easily fixed.

She had to accept that the rape had been real. Given the medical evidence and her state of mind, nothing else made sense. But the truth was still sinking in, too much truth for her ravaged psyche to process. It was as if she was tumbling through a black void with no bottom and nothing of substance to hold on to.

Except Cal.

"It's all right, Megan." His lips brushed her hair as he whispered phrases meant to comfort her. "You'll be fine, girl. You're safe."

Liar, she thought. It wasn't all right—and maybe she would never feel safe again. But she was grateful for the arms that held her, supporting and protecting her. Megan pressed her face into Cal's shirt. The fabric was wet and salty with her tears—real tears. For the first time since that awful night, she was *crying*.

"Go ahead and cry," Cal murmured. "You don't have to be strong all the time. Let it go. I'm here."

She sagged against him, drained by her furious outburst. Cal hadn't meant to hurt her, she reminded herself. He'd only wanted to help. And here, in this remote place, he was all the help she had.

Her knees were threatening to buckle. As if sensing what she needed, Cal swept her up in his arms and carried her to the bed. Throwing back the covers, he laid her on the sheet and tucked the quilt over her, tenderly as if he were tucking in a frightened child.

"Do you want me to go?" he asked.

"No. I need you to stay."

She heard the sound of his boots hitting the floor before he stretched out beside her on top of the quilts. For the first few minutes they lay still, listening to the sounds of the storm. Cal didn't speak, but his weight on the bed and the deep, even cadence of his breathing surrounded her with a sense of peace.

"I still don't remember," she said. "I've no reason to doubt what happened, but the memory isn't there."

"Maybe you're lucky," he said.

"In Darfur, in the camps, I knew so many girls and women who'd been raped by the Janjaweed. It was a form of warfare, a way to shame them and humiliate their families." She turned onto her side, spooning her hips against him. His breath eased out as he laid an arm across her shoulders.

"I used to wonder how they could bear the horror of it," she said. "But somehow they did. They survived and moved on with their lives because they had no choice. They showed so much courage. How can I expect any less of myself? I need to move on, too—and now that I know what happened to me, I will."

"I know you will," he said softly. "You're a strong woman, Megan."

"They're the strong ones. They remember everything—and they don't have a safe place to go to keep it from happening again."

Cal didn't reply, but his arm tightened around her, drawing her closer. The light pressure of her hips set off a rush of sensual warmth. The reaction was nothing she hadn't felt before with Cal. But the fact that it was still there was a surprising comfort. She snuggled closer, feeling his breath quicken in response. The tingling heat spread, flowing into the core of her body to become a subtly throbbing pulse of desire.

She wanted him—with an urgent hunger she'd feared

she would never feel again. But the risk was a fearful one. Another failure would be devastating.

"Cal?" She turned to face him. He was watching her, his silvery eyes tender and questioning. Lifting her hand, she traced a fingertip along his cheek, feeling the soft burn of whisker stubble. "Cal, would you make love to me?"

For what seemed like forever, he didn't reply, didn't even stir. Only a subtle flicker in his eyes betrayed that he'd even heard the question. What if he was about to refuse? The embarrassment would kill her.

One eyebrow quirked. "Are you sure about this?" he asked.

"Yes…" The word barely made it past her trembling lips.

"Then I have a suggestion. Why don't *you* make love to *me?*"

She stared at him, searching his face in the lamplight. Slowly his reasons dawned on her. Let her take control, set the pace, back off if she became uncomfortable. It would be the furthest possible thing from the hellish rape that was locked in her memory.

Did she have the courage to try?

Rising onto her elbows, she leaned over and kissed him—softly at first, letting her lips feather over his, then deepening the contact. As her tongue brushed along the sensitive inner surface of his lower lip, she felt the quiver of his response. She could sense the strain as he willed himself to lie still.

Her mouth nibbled a trail down his throat, tasting the sweet saltiness of his skin. Her caresses barely skimmed the edge of intimacy, but her heart was racing. She could stop anytime, Megan reminded herself. But she didn't want to. All she wanted was Cal, his arms around her and his naked body warming hers.

Tossing her robe aside, she knelt over him. Her fingers, clumsy with haste, fumbled with the buttons of his khaki shirt. So many buttons…

"Let me." He sat up, swung his feet to the floor and in a few easy moves stripped down to his tan silk briefs. With his back toward her, he opened the drawer in the night-stand and withdrew a small packet. The lamplight cast his splendid torso in bronze. The sight of him, and the aware-ness of what was in the packet, kicked Megan's pulse to a thundering gallop. She yanked at the buttons that held her modest pajama top in place.

When he turned around, she was kneeling on the bed, bare to the hips. The way his face lit did wonders to calm her jittery nerves. It told her that he thought she was beau-tiful, and that he wanted her—something she desperately needed to believe.

Hiding the packet under the pillow, he raised the covers and slipped into bed. His heavy-lidded eyes smiled up at her in the shadows. "I can't wait to have you pleasure me," he murmured huskily. "Now, where did we leave off?"

As the storm beat against the bungalow, she stretched out alongside him, aching to touch him, smell him, taste him—every part of him. She wanted to feel alive again—to feel the thrill pulsing through her body and the hot blood coursing through her veins. She wanted to feel joy—with this man.

His mouth was cool and tasted faintly of the single-malt Scotch he'd drunk with Harris. Her tongue darted to meet his in a playful pantomime of what was meant to come. Her bare nipples grazed his chest, lingering until she broke off the kiss and nipped her way down over his collarbone.

As if playing a game with rules, he kept his hands at his sides; but other parts of him were fully responsive. He moaned as her lips closed around his aureole, tongue circling the tiny nub, coaxing it to heat and swell. His flesh was salty after the day in the hot sun, his pungent sweat deliciously male. Even this…it was heaven. She couldn't get enough of him.

As his hips arched against her, she could feel his sex, jutting along her thigh. She shifted, legs parting, pelvis tilting to bring her throbbing center into contact with that rock-solid ridge. Even through layers of fabric she could feel every inch of him. She thrust harder, hungry need spiraling through her body until the gentle press of his hand on her hip stayed her.

"You naughty girl…" he growled. "Do you have any idea what you're doing to me?"

"Yes, and I'm about to do more." The sense of power was intoxicating. Giddy with her newfound courage, she shed her pajama bottoms and panties and slid her hand beneath the waistband of his straining silk briefs. Her pulse leaped as her fingers brushed, then clasped his naked erection. To her touch, he felt as big as a stallion, as hard as a hickory log and as smooth as velvet. A purr of sheer pleasure vibrated in his throat as she stroked him, intensifying her confidence and her desire.

She loved the feeling of him in her hand, but she sensed she was pushing him to his limit. And her own sweet hunger was growing more urgent. She could feel the pulsing of her own need, the slickness of moisture all but dripping from between her thighs. She'd expected to be fearful, or at least hesitant; but all she could think of was how much she wanted him inside her.

Stripping his silk briefs down his legs, she tossed them aside and reached for the condom he'd hidden under the pillow. Slipping it over his firm erection was done in seconds. Cal's lust-glazed eyes held a glint of amusement as he watched her cloak him.

"Are you all right with this, Megan?" he whispered.

She flashed him a grin. "I've never been more all right in my life."

A slow smile spread across his face. "That's good, because you're driving me crazy. I want to be inside you so much I can't stand it."

And that was enough, she thought. No pretty lies about being in love with her. No useless flattery. Nothing was settled between them except that he wanted her. And she wanted him.

Straddling his hips, she found the center of her slickness and lowered herself down the length of his shaft. He filled her, so deep that, as she settled onto him, she could feel his manly heat pulsing through her whole body.

As she began to move, he responded with a groan. Unable to keep still, his hands came into play, clasping her hips as he drove upward into her, thrusting deeper and deeper. Where their bodies joined, shimmering bursts of pleasure ignited inside her. She came, clenching around him as the climax washed over her in waves, leaving her deliciously spent.

"Don't stop," he urged, thrusting again. She matched her motion to his. This time she rode a rocket into the stars, reeling and gasping as his release mounted. He came with her, exploding with a grunt, followed by a long outward breath and a low chuckle of satisfaction.

Still feeling spasms in the depths of her body, Megan sagged over him. She was utterly spent, but she had never felt more free. Only time would tell whether the nightmares would return. But with Cal's help, she had broken the barrier of fear. He had given her hope—and so much more.

Tears of relief and gratitude welled as she leaned forward and brushed a kiss across his smiling lips. "Thank you," she whispered.

* * *

As early dawn crept through the curtains, Cal lay spooned against Megan's sweet nakedness, his hand resting on her hip. The even cadence of her breathing told him she was still fast asleep.

They'd made love again in the night, this time in the more traditional way. Cal had feared that having a man on top of her might awaken her bad memories, but his worries had been unfounded. The second time had been every bit as wonderful and revealing as the first.

She shifted against him, settling her lovely bum deeper into the curve of his body. With a sigh, he tightened an arm around her. He'd enjoyed her beauty and relished her passion. But what moved him most was her trust. That a woman who'd been through hell would give herself to him as Megan had, with nothing held back, stirred emotions Cal had never known he possessed. It was as if he'd been handed a magnificent gift he didn't deserve. He felt unworthy, humbled, overwhelmed.

With Megan he'd ventured to a place where he'd never been with a woman—and it scared the hell out of him.

After last night, the thought of letting her go was more than he could stand. He wanted to protect her from the ugliness in the world. He wanted to heal her pain and see her smile every day—maybe for a long time to come. But questions swarmed at him. What about the past? What about her determination to return to Darfur? And what if he were to find evidence that Megan had embezzled the missing money?

As long as doubt existed on any front, he'd be a fool to trust her. He'd trusted his mother. He'd trusted Nick—trust that he was now beginning to question. The last thing he needed was another betrayal from a person he cared about.

Pulling her closer, he filled his senses with the soft lavender fragrance of her hair. For now, at least, he would be here, giving her the support she needed to heal. As long as she was willing, he would enjoy every minute of their lovemaking.

But he would keep his emotions under tight rein; and he would remember why he'd come to Africa in the first place. No one, not even Megan, would ever deceive him again.

Eleven

Megan woke to the sound of the shower running. For a moment she lay still while her mind processed the realities of her new, changed world. Last night, she'd learned the shocking truth about the rape in Darfur. And later on, when she and Cal had made love, she'd responded with newfound passion. It was as if a dam had burst, forever changing the landscape of her life.

She stretched her naked body in the bed, relishing the aches and twinges she hadn't felt in so very long. She felt like a whole woman again, and she had Cal to thank for it.

Not that she believed she was healed. The brutality she'd experienced would haunt her for the rest of her days. At some point she might remember everything. Even if she didn't, she might need therapy. But she'd turned a corner. She believed and accepted what had happened; and she no longer felt paralyzed by the fears that had taken over her life.

The shower had stopped running. Facing Cal would be one more new reality. Last night they'd become lovers. But what about today? Where would they go from here?

She had no illusions about love. Not with Cal. To a man like him, sex was just sex. And if she allowed herself to want more, she'd only get her heart broken.

But on safari, she couldn't simply get dressed and leave. The two of them would be together twenty-four/seven for most of the next week. Things could become awkward between them. As for the future…but even if she wanted something with him, and even if she could somehow convince him to agree, what kind of future could she expect, given the baggage from their shared pasts?

She was sitting up, reaching for her robe, when the bathroom door opened and Cal stepped out. He was naked except for the white towel that wrapped his hips, his splendid torso gleaming with moisture. Tossing the towel aside, he strode toward the wardrobe and then glanced back at her with a friendly grin. "Rise and shine. Harris wants us out front in thirty minutes."

So it would be business as usual—and that was fine, Megan told herself. Clutching her robe to her chest, she fled toward the bathroom. After flashing in and out of the shower, she finger-combed her hair and slathered her face, neck, arms and hands with sunscreen. By the time she emerged from the bathroom, Cal had dressed and gone out, leaving his packed duffel next to the door, probably for the staff to pick up.

The message was clear. He was keeping his distance.

Had she said or done something wrong? Had last night's performance failed to meet his expectations? Or was he just making it clear that he didn't want to get entangled? Fine, she would follow his example and behave as if nothing had happened between them.

Willing herself to ignore the sting, she finished dressing, closed her duffel and made a last-minute sweep of
the bungalow to make sure nothing had been left behind.
That done, she parked her bag next to Cal's and opened
the front door.

Cal stood on the porch, a grin on his face and a cup of
coffee in each hand. "We've got a few minutes," he said.
"After last night, I thought we might need this to wake up."

Megan's heart rose like a helium birthday balloon as
he put the cups on the outdoor table and turned to pull her
into his arms. His kiss was sweet and tender, lingering
just long enough. Exactly what she needed this morning.
"You're amazing," he whispered in her ear.

"You're pretty amazing yourself," she countered, play-
fully rubbing her head against his chin.

Letting her go, he retrieved the cups and handed her
one. Together they stood on the porch, cradling the warm
cups between their palms and watching the African sunrise
flame across the sky. It was one of those moments made all
the more perfect, Megan thought, because it couldn't last.

"Will you be all right today?" Cal asked her.

"I'll be fine." She took a sip of the hot, rich Tanzanian
brew. "But I'd just as soon not share this situation with
Harris. He'd have far too much fun with it."

"Agreed." He punctuated the word with a chuckle. "I'll
be on my best behavior today. Just so you won't be surprised, we'll be sharing a single tent with two cots for the
next few nights."

"Fine. Something tells me I don't really want to be alone
in a tent on the Serengeti. I have visions of some hungry
hyena wandering in to munch on my leg. You can be there
to chase him away."

"I'll confess that wasn't the first advantage I thought
of." The gray eyes that gazed down at Megan held a slightly

naughty twinkle, and she knew he was thinking about making love to her again. It felt good, knowing he wanted her—even though she knew things might well be different later on. Cal had always been a man with an agenda. He may have put that agenda aside for now, but sooner or later it would resurface. When that happened, it would be as if this romantic interlude had never taken place.

Was she falling in love with him? Was that the reason her brain kept flashing those red warning lights? Cal Jeffords was a compelling man, but Megan knew he didn't hold her blameless for Nick's crime and subsequent suicide. Revenge might not be far from the top of his list. She'd be a fool to lower her guard—but meanwhile she was having such a wonderful time. It was like being Cinderella at the ball—but with the constant awareness that the clock was ticking toward midnight.

By the time they finished their coffee, it was time to meet Harris and Gideon for a quick predeparture breakfast. Cal helped the driver load the last of their gear into the vehicle, and they were off.

They were headed north, toward the Kenyan border where the vast Serengeti Plain spanned the two countries. In the dry season the game herds migrated north in search of water and food. At the start of the long rains, they swept southward by the hundreds of thousands, to graze on the abundant fresh grass and raise their young. It was this grand spectacle that Harris had promised to show them.

As the Land Rover sped along the narrow ribbon of paved road, Cal stole a glance at Megan. She was seated with her arm resting on the back of the seat, the breeze fluttering the green scarf at her throat. He took a moment to feast his eyes on her. True to their understanding, she gave no sign that anything had changed between them. But he couldn't forget that last night she'd been his—quivering above him, her head thrown back, while he exploded deep inside her. Right now, all he could think about was having her again, and soon.

He'd set out to seduce her, and now he'd succeeded, but with more complications than he could've imagined in his wildest dreams. Her beauty was a given. But it was her blend of courage and vulnerability that had hit him with the impact of a ten-ton truck.

She was Nick's widow. Cold reasoning told him he couldn't dismiss her link to the stolen money. But last night she'd given herself to him with all her woman's passion. She'd reached out and trusted him to lead her back from the edge of hell. How could he even think of using that trust to get the answers he wanted? But then, again, how could he not? He'd spent two years searching and had even come to Africa to learn the truth—he wasn't going home without it.

A bump in the road jarred him back to the present. The landscape had opened up into rolling hills, carpeted with pale green shoots of sprouting grass. On a flat rise, a cluster of round huts came into view, with mud walls and artfully thatched, conical roofs. Rangy-looking cattle, watched over by young boys, grazed on the slopes.

"Maasai," Harris explained for Megan's benefit. "They're all over these parts with their cattle and goats, living pretty much like they have for hundreds of years. Back in the old days, do-gooders tried to civilize them. But the rascals didn't take to civilizing. They wanted to keep their spears and their cows and their old ways. They still do."

The Land Rover had come up on a herd of goats, grazing in a hollow where the runoff from the road had nourished the grass. The young boy guarding them showed spindly legs below his crimson togalike garment. He grinned and waved as they passed.

Megan called out *"Jambo,"* laughing as she returned the wave. It was plain to see that she adored children. What a shame she'd never had any of her own. That miscarriage she'd suffered must've been devastating.

"What a beautiful boy," she said.

"Oh, they're a handsome lot, all right," Harris snorted. "And vain as all get-out, especially the so-called warriors. The women do the work, the boys herd the stock, and aside from making babies, the men haven't much to do but strut around with their spears and look pretty."

"Is it still true that a young Maasai has to kill a lion with a spear before he can be called a man?" Cal asked.

Harris guffawed. "Lions are protected these days. But knowing the Maasai, I wouldn't be surprised if it still happens. Years ago I showed up in time to save one of the young fools. His spear had snapped. The lion was about to rip him apart when I stepped in. That's how *this* happened." He nodded toward his pinned-up sleeve.

Megan shot Cal a mischievous glance, rolling her eyes skyward. A smile teased her kissable mouth. She looked luscious enough to devour on the spot. He could hardly wait to get her alone.

He was in over his head—and he knew it.

By the time they arrived at the campsite, it was late in the day. Clouds were rumbling across the vast expanse of sky, threatening a downpour.

Megan had half expected they'd be pitching camp on their own. She should have known better. Harris's competent safari staff had everything set up and waiting for them, including a savory dinner of saffron rice, vegetables and chicken cooked over an open fire.

Set on high ground, safe from flooding, there were tents for staff and guests along with sheltered cooking and eating areas. Megan was astonished to discover that the tent she shared with Cal featured an adjoining bathroom with a flush toilet and a primitive but functional shower.

"Magic!" Harris laughed at her surprise. "We can't have clients wandering out to the loo in the dark, can we? They might not make it back."

After the long, bumpy ride in the Land Rover, it was heavenly to sit in the open front of the dining tent and watch the rain drip off the canvas. The day had been spectacular. They'd seen elephants, giraffes, ostriches and a pride of lions feasting on the zebra they'd killed. White-headed vultures and marabou storks had flocked around them, waiting their turn at the leavings. In this place of raw, cruel beauty, nothing went to waste.

Megan had watched breathless as a cheetah streaked after a gazelle and brought it down in a single bound. Two cubs, hiding in the grass, had scampered out to join their mother at the feast. Death was brutal on the Serengeti, but it nourished new life.

As the darkness deepened, they sat in folding chairs, watching the rain and listening to the sounds of the awakening night—the distant roar of a lion, the titter of a hyena, the cry of a bird and the drone of insects in the grass. Harris sipped his bourbon, lantern light deepening the hollows under his eyes. He looked old and tired, Megan thought. Maybe the life of a safari guide was becoming too strenuous for him.

"Cal already knows this," he said to Megan, "but I need to make it clear for you. Once you go into your tent for the night, you zip the flap and don't open it till you hear the boys in the morning. No traipsing around in the dark, hear? You never know what's going to be out there."

Megan laughed. "Not to worry. No power on earth could drag me out of that tent in the middle of the night."

"Speaking of the tent…" Cal set down his glass, stood and stretched. "I'm ready to turn in. You should get some rest, too, Harris. It's been a long day." He glanced at Megan. Taking her cue, she rose. It had been a tiring day for her, too. But if Cal had lovemaking on his mind, she was on board. Just looking at him was enough to make her ache.

Harris remained in his chair. He really did look tired, Megan thought. Feeling a surge of affection, she bent and kissed the weathered cheek. "Do get some sleep, Harris," she murmured. "We don't want to wear you out tomorrow."

"Thanks for thinking of an old man." Patting her hand, he glanced up at Cal. "You take care of this girl, hear? She's a good one."

"She is, and I'll do that." Switching on a flashlight and opening a handy umbrella, Cal ushered her toward their tent. The storm had subsided to a steady drizzle. Exotic animal sounds, like the track from an old Tarzan movie, filled the night.

"Will it really be dangerous out here," she asked, "or was Harris just trying to scare me?"

"You can take him at his word. The staff will keep a fire going to scare off anything big. But that won't be much help if you walk outside and step on a snake."

Megan shuddered. "That's enough. You've convinced me to behave."

"Behave? You?" Cal teased. "We'll see about that."

They'd reached the sheltered entrance to their tent. Cal laid the umbrella on a chair and checked the interior with the flashlight beam. "All clear," he said. "Come on in."

Megan stepped into the tent and bent to close the long zipper that secured the flap. When she straightened and

turned around, Cal was standing in the narrow space between the cots. In the dim glow of the flashlight, his eyes
held a glint of pure, unbridled lust.

"I've been waiting all day to get my hands on you," he
growled, opening his arms and moving toward her.

Megan met him partway. He crushed her close, his kiss
flaming through her like the tail of a meteor. They tore
at each other's clothes, buttons popping, belts and shoes
thudding. Megan left her slacks wadded on the floor. Still
in her bra and panties, she hooked his hips with one leg,
bringing his erection into hard contact with her aching
sex. Wild with need, she ground against him through his
briefs, heightening the hot sweetness until her head fell
back and she came with a little shudder, ready for more.
She had never felt so free.

"What a little wanton you've turned out to be. Who
knew?" He chuckled under his breath as he unhooked her
bra and tossed it on the cot. His hand slid inside her panties, fingers stroking her, riding on her slickness. "Damn
it, but I want you. All I can think about right now is being
inside you!"

"Would you believe it's all I can think about...too?"
She shed her panties. Her hand tugged at his briefs, pulling them down to free his bulging erection. The cots were
narrow, but that was of little concern as he lowered her
onto the nearest one and slipped on protection before he
mounted her and drove in hard. Megan flung her legs
around his hips, pulling him deeper inside her. She loved
the way his length and thickness filled every inch of her.
She loved the feel of him, gliding silkily along her sensitive
inner surfaces, igniting a trail of sparks that soared through
her body. She met his thrusts, heightening the dizzy spiral
of sensations that carried her with him, mounting upward
to release in a shattering burst.

For a moment he lay still. His breath was warm against her shoulder as he exhaled, chuckled and rolled off the cot.

"Did we break anything?" he teased, grinning down at her.

"Are you asking about me or the bed?" Megan sat up and ran a hand through her damp hair. She felt gloriously spent. "For the record, I believe we're both intact."

He bent and brushed a kiss across her mouth. "You're amazing," he said.

"So you tell me," she responded with a little laugh. "Sometimes I even amaze myself."

They lay awake in the darkness, veiled by mosquito netting and separated by the narrow space between their cots. Outside the tent, the sounds of the African night blended in a symphony of primal nature.

Wrapped in contentment, Megan stretched her legs beneath the blankets. The day had been splendid, the night even more so. She didn't want this time to end. But she knew better than to talk about the future. Here, with the outside world far away, she and Cal had found something memorable. But days from now, she knew, only the memory would remain.

"I wish I could record those sounds outside and take them with me," she said. "The rain, the animals…they'd lull me to sleep anywhere, even in Darfur."

A leaden silence hung between them before he spoke. "You can't mean to say you're still planning to go back!"

"Why not?" Even as she said the words, Megan could feel her resolve crumbling. But she held fast. "I'm feeling so much better now. And those people need me. I can't just turn my back and walk away."

He sat up, a dark silhouette through the mosquito netting that draped his cot. "I'm not asking you to turn your back. I'm asking you to take more time off. Make sure you're strong enough."

"Is that all?" The words slipped out before Megan could stop them. Her heart sank. The last thing she wanted was to question Cal's motives like a whiny, insecure female fishing for a commitment.

"No, it isn't all," he said. "The past few days have been wonderful. I care about you, Megan. I want to see where you and I are headed before I let you go anywhere. Is that so hard to accept?"

Megan's throat had gone dry. Only as Cal's words sank in did she realize how she'd been yearning to hear them. She *wanted* him to care for her. She *wanted* more time with him. But believing those words could get her heart broken. Cal had come to Africa seeking one thing—justice. And he was the sort of man who'd do anything to get what he wanted. That included playing her any way he could.

She found her voice. "I didn't realize we were headed anywhere. What about the money you suspect I took? Isn't that why you came after me?"

He hesitated, as if weighing his reply. "In part—at first. But knowing you as I do now, I can't believe you're hiding anything. You're as transparent as fine crystal, Megan. That's one of the things that I…" He fumbled for the right words. "One of the things I find so compelling about you. And right now I'm here because of *you,* not the damned money."

Megan's heart leaped. She'd wanted to hear those words from him. And now she wanted to believe they were true. But were they? Or was he still manipulating her?

With a weary sigh he lay down again. The cot creaked as he adjusted his tall frame. "So what's it to be? Will you give me more time before you vanish out of my life again?"

Megan gazed up into the darkness, her emotions churning. She wanted this man in more ways than she could name. But did she want him enough to risk heartbreak or betrayal?

"I can't make that decision tonight," she said. "Give me a few days to think about it—maybe until we're headed back to Arusha. All right?"

"All right," he grumbled. "But you can expect some lobbying on my part. I'm not one to take no for an answer."

"I know." Torn, she blinked away a secret tear. "Now, let's get some sleep. Harris will be rousting us out early tomorrow."

He mumbled a reply, already drifting. Megan closed her eyes and soon fell into a dreamless sleep.

It was barely dawn when a commotion outside the tent shocked her awake. Megan sat bolt upright. She could hear the sound of shouts and running feet.

Cal was awake, too. "Stay inside," he said. "I'll see what's happening."

He was pulling on his pants when Gideon's frantic voice came through the closed tent flap. "Open up! We need you!"

"What's wrong?" Cal yanked the zipper down. Gideon's face was ashen.

"Hurry! It's Mr. Harris! I think he's had a heart attack!"

Twelve

Still in her pajamas, Megan raced outside. Harris lay gray-faced and unconscious on the canvas apron in front of his tent. Megan dropped to her knees beside him. He wasn't breathing. No time to check for a pulse. It had to be a heart attack. Willing herself not to panic, she placed her hands at the base of Harris's sternum, shifted her weight above him and fell into the rhythmic compressions of CPR. Her nurse's training had taught her to keep a cool head, but a voice inside her was screaming. This old man had grown dear to her. She couldn't lose him.

Why hadn't she paid more attention to him last night? He'd looked ill even then. If she'd checked him, she might have been able to do something sooner.

Gideon hovered over her, visibly shaken. "He came outside and fell. Is he going to die?"

"Not if I can help it." Megan kept the rhythm steady. "When did this happen?"

"Just before I called you. He has been like a father to me…" Gideon's voice broke.

Megan didn't look up. "Radio the airport in Arusha," she said. "Tell somebody to send a plane with medical equipment. Hurry!"

"No, not Arusha. I know who to call." Gideon raced for the Land Rover, which was equipped with a radio.

Cal had been standing back to give her room. Now he knelt beside her. "I can do this. Let me take over while you make sure the message gets through."

"Thanks." Megan let his hands slip under hers, keeping the rhythm unbroken. That done, she clambered to her feet and raced after Gideon. By the time she reached the vehicle, he was already on the radio, speaking in terse English to a voice that could barely be heard through the crackling static. Ending the call, he turned back to Megan.

"Flying Doctors. We have a contract with them. They can be here in half an hour and take him to Nairobi. Can you keep him alive that long?"

"We can only try." Megan raced back to where she'd left Cal with Harris and gave him the news. She'd heard of the air ambulance company that served much of East Africa, but in her haste to get help she'd forgotten. Thank heaven Gideon had thought to call them.

"That's some hope at least." Cal's strong hands kept up their pumping on Harris's chest. "Go get some clothes on. We can spell each other till the plane gets here." His gaze met Megan's, and she saw the fear that neither of them would voice. There was no way of knowing whether CPR could keep Harris alive. By the time the plane arrived, it could be too late to save him.

Rushing into the tent, she yanked on her clothes and shoved her feet into her boots. As an afterthought, she flung some essentials into her day pack and shoved her passport, with its multiple-entry Kenyan visa, into her pocket. If there was room in the plane, she wanted to be ready to go along. Harris would need someone there who knew him, and as a nurse, she was the logical choice. She would ask Gideon to find Harris's passport, as well. It would at least give the distraught man something to do.

She was closing her pack when she heard Cal's voice calling her. Stumbling over her boot laces, she raced out of the tent. Her heart dropped as she saw that he'd stopped the chest compressions. But then she noticed the relief that glazed his face.

"I'm getting a pulse," he said. "He seems to be coming around."

"Oh, thank God!" Megan dropped to Harris's near side. She saw at once that his color was improving. A touch along the side of his throat confirmed a thready heartbeat. "Water," she called out. "And bring a pillow and blanket!"

Someone handed her a plastic water bottle. Twisting off the cap, Megan wet her hand and smoothed it over Harris's face. He gasped, taking in precious oxygen. His eyelids fluttered open. His mouth worked to form words.

"What the hell…?" he muttered.

"Hush." Megan laid a finger on his parchment-dry lips. "You've had a heart attack, Harris. Lie still. The plane's on its way."

"Feel like I've been kicked by a damned elephant…" He struggled vainly to sit up.

"Stay put, *mzee*." Cal's hands on his shoulders held him gently in place. "You almost checked out on us. We want to keep you around."

Someone handed Megan the bedding she'd asked for. She tucked the blanket around Harris and slid the pillow under his head. He still looked as frail as a snowflake. The plane would be sure to carry oxygen and a defibrillator;

but until it arrived, the old hunter could go back into cardiac arrest at any time. All they could do was keep him quiet and hope for the best.

Lifting his head, she held the water bottle to his lips. "Just enough to wet your mouth," she cautioned. "And then I'm going to give you an aspirin to chew."

"Water and aspirin!" He swore in protest. "Hell, give me a swig of bourbon and let me up. I'll be as good as new!"

Megan exchanged worried looks with Cal. The old man's spunk was definitely back. But that didn't mean the danger was any less grave. In fact, he could put himself in danger if he refused to settle down. While she held his sunburned hands, her eyes gazed anxiously at the sky. Nairobi, the capital of Kenya, was only about fifty air miles away—closer than Arusha. Gideon had promised that the doctors would arrive in half an hour, but she hadn't thought to check her watch. How much longer did they have to wait?

The minutes crawled past. In a blessedly short time, they heard the drone of a small aircraft. Megan breathed a prayer of thanks as the single-engine Cessna landed on a level strip of ground below the camp. Within minutes Harris was hooked up to oxygen, strapped to a stretcher and on his way to the plane.

Megan, who'd been given the OK to come along, followed with her day pack slung on her shoulder. With one backward glance at Cal, she swung into the plane and took the last empty seat. There'd been no time to say goodbye. She would likely see him again in Nairobi, but their interlude in this African paradise was over. Whatever happened between them now would happen amid the stresses and uncertainties of the real world.

Cal watched the departing plane until it vanished into the sunrise. Harris was in capable hands, he told him-

self. Kenyatta Hospital in Nairobi was modern and well
equipped, its doctors as competent as any in Africa. As
for Megan, it had been the right decision for her to go. But
there was a cold hollow inside him where her warmth had
been. He hadn't planned on her being torn from him so
soon—or so abruptly, without so much as a chance to say
goodbye. Only now that she was gone did he realize how
empty he felt without her.

He would see her at the hospital, of course, but under
strained conditions. They would both be concerned about
Harris and focused on his needs. There'd be little opportunity for them to be alone or to make any decisions about
their budding relationship.

Budding? Was that what it was? He'd scarcely spent
a week with Megan, but now that she was gone he felt
damned near lost without her. What was that supposed
to mean?

But that thought would have to wait. Right now he had
other urgent concerns on his mind.

The plan was for Cal and Gideon to load the personal
gear in the Land Rover, drive back to Arusha and make
the flight from there to Nairobi in Cal's corporate jet. It
was the course of action that made the most sense. With
Megan gone, Cal had no more reason to stay in Arusha.
And Gideon was the closest thing to family the old man
had. In Nairobi, he could look after Harris's needs and see
him home after his release from the hospital.

Cal would see that Gideon had plenty of money for his
lodging, meals and transportation. He would also make
sure there'd be no problem with Harris's medical expenses.
He could afford it, and it was at least one way he could
help.

Nairobi might also be his last chance to arrive at an understanding with Megan. Things had been good between

them last night. But she still seemed set on returning to Darfur. He'd told her he wanted more time together, but even though she'd agreed to consider the idea, they no longer had the luxury of the rest of their safari to decide what would come next. If he was going to convince her to give him a real chance, he'd have to move very fast. Maybe he needed to open up and tell her how he really felt. Otherwise he could lose her for good—and he wasn't ready to let that happen.

"Hello, sweetheart." Harris was sitting partway up, an oxygen line hooked to his nose. Above the bed, monitors attached to his body flickered and beeped.

"Hello, you old rogue." Megan stepped to his bedside and brushed a kiss across his forehead. His color was much improved, and his eyes had recovered a bit of their twinkle, but he was far from out of the woods. A few hours ago the doctors had performed an angioplasty to clear out the clogged artery that had caused his heart attack. The attending physician had told her his chances for recovery were good, but only if he took better care of his health.

"Where's Cal?" he asked her.

"Cal and Gideon are driving to Arusha and flying from there. Unless they've been delayed, they should be here by tonight."

"Gideon's coming? Good."

"He wanted to be here. He said you were like a father to him."

"The rascal would only say that if he thought I was dying." Harris snorted dismissively, but something in his voice told Megan the old man had been touched.

"The doctor's going to come in to lecture you soon," Megan said, taking a seat next to the bed. "If you don't want to end up back in the hospital, you're going to have to make some changes. No more smoking. Cut way back on alcohol and red meat—"

"Oh, bother! Will he say I have to give up all those women who are chasing me, too?"

"You're incorrigible."

"And you're the sweetest thing to come into my life since I don't know when." His hand brushed Megan's cheek. "If I was thirty years younger and if Cal hadn't already staked his claim on you—"

"Staked his claim? Maybe he should ask me first."

"He will if you stick around. I've noticed the way he looks at you. The man's so lovesick he can barely lace his boots. Hellfire, girl, I do believe you're blushing."

"I haven't blushed since I was fifteen years old." But Megan's face did feel unsettlingly warm. Was Harris right about Cal? Surely the old man was teasing her. How could she let herself believe that? "Let's talk about something else," she said.

He looked thoughtful. "Well, I guess I could thank you for saving my life."

"I can't take credit for that. It was Cal who did most of the CPR and Gideon who called the plane."

"But you're the one who stayed with me and talked me into hanging on. So just for you, I've a confession to make." His pale blue eyes twinkled mysteriously. "I've been filling your pretty head with tall tales about how I lost my arm. If you promise to keep it a secret, I'll tell you the real story."

"You mean it wasn't a jealous husband or a rhino or a lion? This, I need to hear. Certainly I'll keep your secret." Megan leaned closer to the bed. "I promise."

"It was back in England," he said. "My family was dirt poor, with six mouths to feed. I was fifteen when I quit school to work in a coal mine. The place was a black hellhole. But it was the only job to be had for a boy like me.

One day a slab of coal fell out of the ceiling and crushed my arm. The flesh and bone were too far gone to heal, and there was no money for a doctor. When gangrene set in, the local butcher got me drunk and cut off the arm to save my life."

"Oh…" Megan gazed at him in dismay. No wonder Harris made up those fanciful stories about losing his arm. The real story was too sad to share with clients. "What did you do, Harris? How did you survive?"

"I'd always been good with a gun. It took some practice, but I learned to shoot one-armed with my father's old army rifle. To feed the family, I started poaching deer and grouse off the local estate. Got caught, of course. Barely escaped with my hide. Stowed aboard a freighter and ended up in Africa. No papers—but it was easier to get by in those days."

"That's quite a story, Harris." Cal stood in the doorway, looking rumpled and weary in the clothes he'd pulled on that morning. "I've always wondered about it myself. Trust Megan to charm the truth out of you."

The old hunter smiled, but it was plain to see that so much talking had tired him. Megan watched Cal as he crossed the room toward her. They'd been apart for only a few hours, but now that he was here she realized how much she'd missed him.

"Harris swore me to secrecy," she said. "Since you were listening, you have to swear, too. Not a word."

"Consider it done. My lips are sealed." Cal's hand brushed across her shoulder as he moved to the head of the bed. She felt his touch through her shirt and along her skin like the passing of a warm breeze. After the long, stressful day, the need to be in his arms was compelling enough to hurt.

The look he gave Harris betrayed how worried he'd been. "You gave us quite a scare, old friend," he said.

"Oh, I'll be fine." Harris winked. "Just might have to cut back on my bad habits, that's all. Where's Gideon? Didn't he come?"

"Gideon's down in the cafeteria grabbing a sandwich. He wants to sit with you tonight, so I suggested he eat first. Meanwhile, I hope you won't mind if I take Megan back to the hotel for some dinner and a good night's rest. We can stay till Gideon gets here."

Harris waved them away. "Go on. I'll be fine. There's this good-looking nurse on duty. If I'm alone when she comes in, maybe I can get somewhere with her."

Cal shook his head. "Just don't overdo it, you old rascal! We'll see you later."

Megan rose, blew Harris a farewell kiss and allowed Cal to escort her out of the room. His hand rested lightly on the small of her back as they walked through the maze of hallways and took the elevator to the hospital lobby. "I booked us a room at the Crowne Plaza." He named one of the city's premier luxury hotels. "Your things are there, and we have reservations in the dining room. I'm guessing you'll be hungry."

"Starved. But I'll settle for something quick in the coffee shop. I look a fright, and I'm too tired to get cleaned up for dinner."

The Crowne Plaza was an easy drive from Kenyatta Hospital, but the cab took time to weave its way through the tangle of evening traffic. Too tired to talk, Megan stared out the cab windows at the busy streets. She was no stranger to the big, bustling city of Nairobi. It was the jumping-off point for the refugee camps in northern Kenya and the Sudan. If she decided to go back to Darfur from here, it shouldn't be too difficult to find transportation.

But when it came to that decision, her heart was still torn. She was needed in Darfur. And going back might help her face her buried fears. But she'd found something warm and thrilling with Cal—something she realized she'd been searching for all her life. If there was a chance it might last, she'd be tempted to stay. But she'd known Cal too long not to have doubts. Was he really capable of a long-term relationship—with anyone, much less her—or was he still just a man with an agenda?

The taxi was slowing down, turning left into the hotel driveway. Other times in Nairobi, Megan had ridden local buses and stayed at one of the cheap boardinghouses frequented by volunteers like her. Now as the cab pulled up to the elegant, ultramodern complex, she felt as if she'd stumbled into a different world. The old Megan would have been right at home here. But that woman was gone forever. She was a different person now.

But when he looked at her, which woman did Cal see?

The hotel coffee shop was too noisy for serious conversation. Cal studied Megan across the table as she finished the last of her chicken and rice and sipped her mineral water. He'd planned a romantic evening in a setting where he could lay his heart on the line. But he should have known it wasn't the best idea. Megan had been rousted out of bed by Harris's heart attack, flown with him in the plane and remained at the hospital for the rest of the day. Stress showed in every line and shadow of her face. What she needed tonight was rest, not romance.

They rode the elevator up to their room, having conversed mostly about Harris, the flight, his surgery and recovery. "You look worn out," Cal said as she surveyed the room with its king-size bed. "Your duffel's on that bench by the wall. The bathroom's all yours."

"Wonderful. I could really use a shower." She rummaged in her bag, pulled out a few things and then vanished into the bathroom. Minutes later the shower came on.

Cal had retrieved his laptop from the plane. The device was functional here in the hotel, and he needed to catch up on his messages. He scrolled through his in-box, marking some for reply, deleting others. What he'd hoped to see was some word from Harlan Crandall about his search for the missing funds. Knowing where the money had gone might at least give him some closure, so he could move ahead with Megan. But there was nothing.

Impatient, he pecked out a message to Crandall asking for an update. By the time he'd finished, the shower had turned off. A moment later, Megan emerged in a cloud of steam. Wrapped in one of the hotel's oversized terry robes, she was damp, glowing and so beautiful it stopped his breath.

"Better?" he asked, finding his voice.

"Better. It's been a long day and I'm done in." She began rubbing her hair dry with a towel, fluffing and curling it with her fingers. The sight of her stirred Cal to a pleasant arousal. Although he'd planned to let her rest, the thought of Megan's fresh, naked body in his arms was giving him different ideas. But he'd had a long day, too, and he didn't exactly smell like a rose garden. He needed a shower before he shared her bed.

With a murmured excuse, he walked into the bathroom, stripped down, turned on the water and lathered his body. The shower took about ten minutes, drying off a few more. With his hips wrapped in a towel, he stepped out of the bathroom.

His anticipation sagged. Megan was curled under the covers on the far side of the bed, deep in slumber.

* * *

Megan stirred and opened her eyes. The last thing she remembered was lying awake, waiting for Cal to finish his shower and join her—for lovemaking, serious talk or whatever was meant to happen. But she'd been so sleepy, she had no memory of his even coming to bed.

Now it was full daylight, and Cal was nowhere to be seen. Only his bag on the luggage stand gave any indication that he hadn't gone for good. Sitting up, she found a note penned on hotel stationery and tucked under the clock on the nightstand.

Good morning, sleepyhead. I didn't have the heart to wake you before I left for the hospital. Since Gideon didn't call me in the night, I'm guessing Harris is fine. If he's not, you'll hear. I'll check back with you later. Meanwhile, please relax and order some breakfast. C.

Megan glanced at the clock. It was almost 9:00 a.m. How could she have slept so late? Flinging aside the covers, she sprang to her feet, then realized her mistake. Lying down for so long and getting up so fast had left her slightly dizzy. Tottering toward a chair, she banged her knee on a small side table. She managed to right the table before it fell, but as it tilted, an object crashed to the floor.

Megan bent to pick it up and recognized Cal's laptop. *Oh, no!* What if she'd broken it?

Worried, she gave the device an experimental shake. Nothing sounded loose, but she noticed that the screen had come on. Maybe Cal had left it in sleep mode—not that she had enough technical savvy to be certain. It appeared he'd been checking his email earlier. His in-box was still open on the screen.

Something popped up on the screen, drawing her eye automatically. It was a "new email" notification letting him know a message had arrived, from someone named

Harlan Crandall. Megan would have dismissed it as none of her business—but then she saw the subject line.

Re: Update on missing foundation funds

Her pulse lurched. The right thing would be to ignore the message. But this concerned *her,* and might even have some bearing on her relationship with Cal. She couldn't *not* look at it.

Racked with guilt for snooping, she highlighted the message and clicked it open.

Dear Mr. Jeffords:

You asked for an update on my investigation. I fear I have little to report. I've traced Mr. Rafferty's activities during the weeks before his suicide, but aside from some large bank withdrawals, I've found nothing that might lead us to the money.

What have you been able to learn from Mr. Rafferty's widow? If we can put our findings together, maybe some new pieces of this puzzle will emerge.

Yours truly,

Harlan Crandall

As Megan laid the laptop back on the table, a strange numbness crept over her. So Cal's motive hadn't changed. He'd pretended to care about her, but all he'd really wanted was to track down the money and prove her guilt. His tenderness, his loving patience—it had all been an act to win her trust.

At least she knew. And she knew what she had to do.

Willing herself to move, not think, she emptied her duffel on the bed and began repacking the contents for a long, rough trip.

Thirteen

Cal's gut clenched as he reread the note Megan had left in the hotel room. It was penned in a shaky script—his only clue to her anguished state of mind.

> *Dear Cal,*
> *By the time you read this I'll be on my way back to Darfur. Now that my decision is made, there's no point in staying, or in drawn-out goodbyes. And there's no point in explaining why I decided to leave. I think you already know.*

Yes, he did know. He'd just seen Crandall's message on his laptop and realized it had been opened and read. Lord, he could just imagine what Megan thought of him now.

> *Don't bother coming after me. I've told you the truth all along—I endorsed the checks and gave them to Nick, and that's all I know. You won't learn anything*

new by tracking me down again, and you won't find the money. I truly believe Nick spent it all. If he hadn't, he'd have given it back when he was caught.

Please give my best to Harris and Gideon. Tell them if I get back to Arusha I'll pay them a visit. Whatever your motives may have been, Cal, I can't leave without thanking you. You did some good things for me. But now it's time for me to go back to where I'm needed. I'm strong enough now. I'll be fine.

There was no closing or signature, as if Megan had put so much emotion into the message that she'd been too drained to finish it.

Cal's first impulse was to go after—find her, drag her back by force if need be and convince her she was wrong about him.

Convince her, damn it, that he was in love with her!

But he knew it wouldn't work. Even if he could track Megan down, forcing her to come back wouldn't be an act of love. It would be an act of control. Megan had made her choice. If he loved her, he would respect that choice— even though letting her go was like ripping out his heart.

He would go home to San Francisco, Cal resolved. There, he would do whatever it took to find out what Nick had done with the stolen funds. The answer had to be somewhere—and when he found it, he would take the evidence and lay it at Megan's feet. Once he could prove her innocence, all the civil suits would go away. It would be safe for her to come home. Maybe then she would forgive him.

Meanwhile, as she faced danger in a savage land, he could only pray that the heavenly powers would keep her safe.

Darfur, two months later

Megan filled her mug with hot black coffee and seated herself at the empty table in the volunteer kitchen. It was early dawn, the sun not yet risen behind the barren hills. But outside the infirmary, the camp was already stirring to life. Through the open window she could hear the crow of a rooster, the cry of a baby and the chatter of women going for water. The familiar scent of baking *kisra,* a Sudanese bread made from ground sorghum, drifted on the air.

Two months after her return to the camp, it was as if she'd never left. Some of the volunteers had moved on, including the doctor who'd diagnosed her rape and filled out the report. But the refugees were mostly the ones she remembered. In a way it was almost like coming home.

The long days kept her blessedly busy. It was only at night that she had time to think about Cal. The man had schemed to win her trust and get information. He had used her shamelessly, and she had let him. She knew she ought to put him out of her mind. But as she lay on her cot in the darkness, the hunger to be in his arms was a soul-deep pain that never left.

"You're up bright and early." Sam Watson, the new doctor, wandered in and filled his coffee cup. He was African-American, middle-aged, with a wife and college-age children back in New Jersey. Megan had warmed at once to his friendly manner.

"This is my favorite part of the day," Megan said. "The only time it's calm around here."

"I understand. Can I get you something before I sit

down? Some eggs? Some nice fried Spam?" He lifted the cover off the electric fry pan where the Sudanese cook had left breakfast to warm.

Megan shook her head. "Coffee's fine."

He filled his plate and sat down across from her. The smell of fried meat triggered a curdling sensation in her stomach.

"You've been off your feed lately." He stirred a packet of sugar into his coffee. "Everything all right?"

"Fine." She forced a smile, clenching her teeth against a rising wave of nausea.

"You're sure? You look a little green this morning. I'd be happy to check you out before we open for business."

"I'm fine. Just need some…air." Abandoning her coffee cup, she rose and stumbled out the back door. The morning breeze was still cool. She gulped its freshness into her lungs.

It couldn't be. It just couldn't be.

But she remembered now that she'd had her last period in Arusha—a week before Cal showed up. That had been more than two months ago.

No, it couldn't be. They'd used protection.

But now she remembered seeing the wrapper on the pack of condoms—a local brand, not known for reliability. Oh, Lord, she should have warned him. But at the time, that had been the last thing on her mind.

"Megan?"

She turned to find the doctor standing behind her.

"I'll be fine, Sam. Just give me a minute."

"I've got something else to give you," he said. "Found a stash of them in the supply closet. Something tells me you might need one of these."

He handed her a small, cellophane-wrapped box. Megan's stomach flip-flopped as she saw the label.

It was a home pregnancy test.

* * *

Megan lay on her cot, staring up into the darkness. One hand rested lovingly on her belly, where the precious new life was growing.

Her baby. Cal's baby. The wonder of it sent a thrill through her body. Two weeks after discovering her pregnancy, she was still getting used to the idea. Only one thing was certain. She wanted this child with all her heart, and she would do anything to keep her little one safe.

When, if ever, would she inform Cal? She supposed he had a right to know. But after the way he'd used her in an effort to glean information, did she want him in her life… or in their child's life?

Cal *would* be in her life, she knew, probably trying to control every aspect of his child's existence—and hers.

She'd learned that Cal could be a genuinely caring person, but his version of caring usually meant taking over. She could do without the Cal Jeffords Master-of-the-Universe brand of caring. But did she have the right to raise her child without a father—and without the advantages that such a father could provide?

So many decisions to make. However, as much as it weighed on her, the question of Cal was far removed from her present world. For now, there were more urgent matters to deal with.

Given her history of miscarriage, Sam had wisely insisted that she be evacuated on the next available plane, which would be arriving with mail and supplies the day after tomorrow. For the near future she could be posted to Arusha, where there was a small modern hospital and ready transportation out of the country. Sooner or later, Megan knew, she would have to face going back to America, where she had no home, no family, no job, few friends who'd remained loyal to her and a stack of legal charges waiting for her. When the time came, involving Cal and his lawyers might be her only choice if she wanted to spend the last stages of her pregnancy anywhere other than inside a courtroom. But for now she wanted to stay in Africa.

She'd asked Sam to keep her pregnancy out of his report, citing simply "health reasons" for her transfer. He'd agreed to her request without demanding the reason.

The hour was late and she'd worked a long day. As she closed her eyes, she could feel herself beginning to drift. Soon she was deep in dreamless sleep.

"Miss Megan! Wake up!" The whisper penetrated the fog of Megan's slumber. She could feel a small hand shaking her shoulder. "Miss Megan…it's me."

Megan opened her eyes. A delicate face, surrounded by the folds of a head scarf, peered down at her. *No! She had to be dreaming!*

"It's me, Miss Megan. It's Saida!"

Still groggy, Megan rolled onto one elbow. "You can't be alive," she muttered. "I saw the Janjaweed—"

"Yes, they took me. For many days they kept me with them. But no more. Now I need you to come."

Megan sat up and switched on the flashlight she kept next to her cot. Yes, it was Saida. But a very different Saida from the innocent girl who'd sneaked out of camp to meet a boy. There was a grim purpose to the set of her mouth, a glint of steel in the lovely doe eyes that had seen too much. Slung over her shoulder by a leather strap was an AK-47 automatic rifle.

"I need you to come," she repeated. "My friend is hurt. I need you to save her."

"You need the doctor. Let me get him."

"No. Not a man. Only you."

None of this was making sense. "Where is your friend? Can't you bring her here?"

Saida shook her head. "Too far. Our camp is in the mountains. I have horses outside. If we ride hard, we can be there by sunrise."

"Saida, I'm going to have a baby," Megan protested. "I can't ride hard."

"We will have to take more time, then." The girlish voice had taken on an edge. "But my friend has been shot. I must bring you or she will die. I made a promise."

Only then did Megan realize what was at stake. Saida had made a desperate vow, and she had a weapon. Megan's choice was to go willingly, as a friend, or be taken at gunpoint. If she tried to warn Sam he might try to stop her, and somebody could get hurt.

"All right." She rose from the bed. "Give me a few minutes to get dressed and gather some medical supplies."

Saida pulled the blanket off Megan's bed and draped it over her arm. "I'll be out back with the horses. Can I trust you?"

"You can trust me," Megan replied, meaning it. She and Saida had shared a hellish experience—the girl's far worse, even, than her own. For good or for ill, the horror of that night had bonded them for life.

As she pulled on her clothes, she glanced at the clock. It was 1:20, no more than five hours before sunrise. At least the camp must not be far away. But if they took more time, as Saida had said, the sun would be well above the horizon before they arrived.

In the supply closet, she dropped bandages, disinfectant, forceps, a scalpel, antibiotics and other needs into a pillowcase. A hastily scrawled note told Sam she'd gone to the aid of a patient in the nearby mountains, and that she'd gone willingly. She could only hope Saida would bring her back before the plane arrived tomorrow afternoon to fly her out of Darfur.

Saida had said her friend was shot. Megan had assisted with treating gunshot wounds, so she knew what needed to be done. But this time she'd be flying blind. She had no idea how badly Saida's friend was hurt, what complications the injury involved, or what would happen if she couldn't save her.

She found Saida waiting with two horses. The girl had folded the blanket and slipped it under Megan's saddle for a more cushioned ride—a gesture that reassured Megan of her good intentions. Still, she sat on the horse gingerly, ever mindful of her unborn baby.

They rode out of the camp in silent single file. Only when they were far out of hearing did Saida pull back, allowing them to ride abreast.

"I saw what they did to you that night," the girl said. "The Janjaweed made me watch before they took me away. I promised to go with them and do whatever they wanted if they left you alive."

Tears burned Megan's eyes as the words sank in. The idea that her life had been saved by the courage of this fifteen-year-old brutalized child clenched around her heart. Speechless for the moment, she reached across the distance between them and squeezed the thin shoulder.

"Thank you," she whispered, finding her voice. "I didn't know."

"When Gamal died it was as if I died, too. For a long time I didn't care what happened to me."

"How did you get away?"

The beat of silence was broken only by the sound of plodding hooves and the distant yelp of a jackal. In the east, the stars had begun to fade against the purple sky. When Saida spoke again her words were a taut whisper. "I was rescued by a band of women who had escaped the Janjaweed. Now we fight to save others."

Megan stared at her young friend, stunned by the revelation. While she had retreated into nightmares, little
Saida, who'd suffered far worse, had used her pain to become a warrior. Falcon fierce, falcon proud—what a lesson
in resilience. Never again, Megan vowed, would she allow
herself to become the prisoner of her own fear.

Saida glanced at Megan's still-slender body. "Your baby
is not Janjaweed?"

"No."

"Where is the father?"

"In America, as far as I know. We are…separated."
The words triggered an unexpected ache. Megan glanced
down at her hands, fighting the emotions that threatened
to unleash a rush of tears. Hearing the despair in Saida's
voice when she spoke of her lost love had Megan questioning the decision she'd made back in Nairobi. Should
she have given Cal more of a chance? She'd been hurt and
shocked by his apparent betrayal…but she hadn't shown
much greater faith in him. Had her leaving been justified,
or had it been triggered by hurt pride? Would she have
made a different decision if she'd known she was carrying Cal's child?

"You loved him." It wasn't a question.

"Yes, I loved him." And she loved him still, Megan realized. She loved Cal, but she'd fled from him at the first
flicker of distrust, giving him no chance to explain himself. Her fear had taken over yet again—the fear of being
hurt the way Nick had hurt her.

What a fool she'd been—and now it was too late. Cal
Jeffords was a proud man, not inclined to give second
chances. Once he learned she was pregnant she could expect him to take an interest in their child, but he would
never trust her again.

The way had narrowed, forcing them to ride single file

once more. With Saida in the lead, they wound through the barren hills, picking their way over loose rock slides and following windswept ridges. As sunrise slashed the sky with crimson, a sense of unease crept over her. She owed Saida her life, and she'd had no choice except to come; but she was riding into an explosive situation where anything could happen. She and her baby could already be in mortal danger.

If she could reach out to Cal now, half a world away, what would she say? Would she tell him she was sorry, or would it be enough just to tell him she loved him?

But what difference would it make? Cal was a proud man, and she'd walked out on him without even saying goodbye—just as his mother had. He would never forgive her.

Geneva, Switzerland

The three-day Conference on World Hunger had given Cal the chance to make some useful connections, but little else. During the long rhetoric-filled meetings, he'd found his mind wandering—always to Megan.

Almost three months had passed since that morning in Nairobi, when he'd come back to the hotel to find her gone; and every time he thought of it, he still felt as if he'd been kicked in the gut. He'd been ready to open up to her, to lay his heart on the line. But Megan had completely blindsided him.

The worst of it was, he couldn't say he blamed her.

He'd resolved to leave her alone until he found proof of what Nick had done. That search had proved a dead end, even for Harlan Crandall. But what did it matter? She'd never asked him to clear her name—she'd just asked him to trust her. And he hadn't. Instead, he'd let a stupid misunderstanding drive her away. He couldn't blame her if she never wanted to see him again.

Now, with the conference over, he leaned back in the cab and closed his tired eyes. He'd dared to hope that, given time, Megan would come around and contact him. The volunteer roster indicated she was still in Darfur, but he'd heard nothing from her. Maybe it was just because she'd washed her hands of him. But he couldn't ditch the feeling that something was amiss. When he'd checked with the travel coordinator, he'd learned that she was being evacuated to Arusha for health reasons. Had she caught some sickness in the camps? Had her nightmares and panic attacks returned? The more he thought about her, the more concerned he became.

The corporate jet was waiting at the airport, fueled and ready to fly him home to San Francisco. Cal thought about the long, dreary flight and lonely return. He thought about Africa and worried about Megan.

He made his decision.

By the morning of the next day, Halima, Megan's sixteen-year-old patient, was alert and wanting breakfast. Two days ago, she'd been shot in the thigh during a skirmish with the Janjaweed. The bullet had gone deep, barely missing the bone. Without medical treatment she would have suffered a lingering death from infection. Megan had removed the slug, cleaned the wound and dosed the stoic girl with antibiotics. Thank heaven she'd been able to save this one.

Megan had sat with the girl most of the night, on a worn rug in an open-sided tent. When she rose at dawn to stretch her legs, she was so sore-muscled she could barely stand. Wincing with each step, she tottered into the open.

The little band of female guerillas had set up their camp

in a brushy mountain glade, near a spring. Megan counted fifteen of them—all young, some no older than Saida. The toughened faces below their head scarves bore invisible scars of what they'd endured. All were armed with knives and AK-47 rifles.

Saida had explained to her how they lived, raiding weapons, horses and supplies from ambushed Janjaweed and accepting gifts of food from grateful refugees. Some of the rescued girls eventually went home to their families. Others like Saida, who had no families, chose to stay with the little band.

"Come with me." Saida was beside her, taking her arm. "I'll get you something to eat and a place to rest. The others can tend to Halima now."

Crouching by the coals of the fire, she uncovered two iron pots. Taking a piece of *kisra* from one, she wrapped it around a scoop of seasoned meat, most likely goat, and thrust it toward Megan. The spicy smell made Megan's stomach roil, but she forced herself to eat it. She was going to need her strength.

"Now that Halima's doing better, I'm hoping we can start back," she said. "I'm due to fly out on the supply plane this afternoon."

But Saida shook her head. "We can't leave till it gets dark. The Janjaweed have eyes everywhere. If they saw us leave here by daylight, they could follow our trail back to this camp."

Megan's heart sank. "So unless the plane is late, I'm going to miss it."

"Yes. I'm sorry." Saida reached out and took her hand. "I understand you need a safe place for your baby. And I can tell you want to be with your baby's father again. But wherever you are, this man you love, if he is worthy of you, he will find you and make you his."

Megan squeezed the thin, brown fingers. If only she could believe those words were true. But when she'd walked out on Cal, she'd closed a door that would never be open to her again.

Fourteen

Cal had hoped to take off for Africa at once, but storms delayed his flight from Geneva till the next morning. It was late that night when the Gulfstream touched down in Nairobi, once more in a heavy downpour.

After a few restless hours in a nearby hotel, he was up by dawn and back at the airport, looking for a small plane to take him to the Darfur camp, where the jet couldn't safely land. The twice-monthly flight that carried medical supplies and mail for the volunteers had gone and returned earlier that day. When found and questioned, the pilot, who knew Megan, said she'd been at the site on earlier trips, but this time he hadn't seen her.

Cal's vague sense of foreboding had burgeoned into a gnawing dread. He could try to call, he supposed, or radio, or however the hell one was supposed to communicate with that place. But he knew that nothing would satisfy him short of going to the refugee camp in person. He had to find Megan, or at least find out what had become of her.

By the time he'd arranged to commandeer the supply plane and pay for a second flight, another storm had moved in, drenching Nairobi in gray sheets of rain. With the flight put off till morning, Cal paced his hotel room, glaring out at the deluge that was keeping him from the woman he loved.

Why had he let her go? He'd told himself that she had the right to make her own choices. But if something had happened to Megan because he hadn't found her in time, he would never forgive himself.

If he found her—no, *when* he found her—and if she'd have him, he would never let her go again.

The ride through the hills was taking even longer than Megan had expected. She and Saida had mounted up after dark and wound their way down the treacherous path to the open plain below. Ever mindful of the danger to her unborn baby, she'd clung to the saddle, silently praying as the trail skimmed sharp ledges in the dark. There was no chance of catching the supply plane now. By the time they reached the refugee camp, it would be long gone. But now she was just hoping they'd reach the camp safely, without any attacks in the night.

With dawn streaking the sky, Saida reined to a halt. Her girlish body stiffened in the saddle as she listened. Megan could hear nothing except the wind, but she saw Saida's mouth tighten. "Janjaweed," the girl said. "Not far, and they're coming fast. We will have to go another way, longer but safer. Follow me and be quiet."

Megan followed Saida's horse up and over a steep ridge. Somewhere behind them she could picture the Janjaweed, arrogant as red-turbaned kings on their swift-moving camels. Saida had her AK-47, but a single girl with a rifle would be no match for the Devil Riders.

Once more Megan said a silent prayer for their safety. She wanted to live. She wanted to hold her baby in her arms. And she wanted another chance to see Cal again.

Would he forgive her for leaving? Or was it too late to mend what she'd broken?

As soon as Cal stepped out of the plane, his worst fears were confirmed. He recognized Dr. Sam Watson from his personnel photo. Tall and balding, his face a study in sleepless concern, he was waiting next to the graveled runway. Megan, who would surely have come out to meet the plane, was nowhere to be seen.

"Megan's gone missing," the doctor said after a hurried introduction. "She left a note, but I've been worried sick, about her—especially since she's pregnant."

"She's...*pregnant?*" Cal's throat clenched around the word.

"Coming up on three months. You look even more surprised than she did." The doctor gave Cal a knowing look. "Would it be presumptuous of me to ask if you're the father?"

The father. Still in shock, Cal forced himself to breathe. This was no time to weigh the implications of what he'd heard. All that mattered now was that Megan was missing in a dangerous place, and she was carrying his child.

"Tell me everything you know," he demanded. "Whatever's happened, I'm not leaving Darfur without her."

Sam was staring past him, into the distance. "You may not have to. Look."

Turning, Cal followed his gaze. Beyond the far end of the runway two mounted figures had come into sight, one small and dressed in native robes, the other taller, wearing a khaki shirt, her light brown curls blowing in the wind.

As she and Saida approached the clinic, the first thing Megan noticed was the plane, which should have departed yesterday. Then she saw the tall, broad-shouldered figure on the landing strip next to Sam Watson.

Her heart slammed. She'd ached to see Cal again, but now that he was here she was suddenly afraid. Had he found more "evidence" against her back home? Was he here to make her pay, as he'd threatened to do at the funeral?

At the end of the runway, Megan slid out of the saddle. Part of her wanted to run to him, but she was sore from riding and dreading the first words he might say to her. She kept her pace to a measured walk while she struggled to build her courage.

Cal was striding toward her, but not running. He seemed to be holding himself back. When they met in the middle of the airstrip, he faced her with his arms at his sides.

Megan forced herself to meet his gaze. He looked exhausted, she thought. The shadows under his eyes had deepened since she'd last seen him.

"Why didn't you let me know about the baby, Megan?" he demanded.

"I only just found out myself."

"Did you ever plan to tell me?"

"Of course I did." She could feel herself beginning to crumble. Her eyes were beginning to well. "This baby is your child, too. How could I not tell you?" A tear escaped to trickle down her cheek.

Something seemed to shatter in him. "Oh, damn it, Megan!" he muttered, and caught her close.

For a long moment she simply let him hold her. Only now did she realize how much she'd wanted to be in his arms.

"Are you all right?" His stubbled chin scraped her forehead as he spoke.

"I've never been more all right in my life." Her arms went around him.

"And our baby?"

"Fine," she whispered. "I should have warned you about those condoms."

"Then I suppose it's time we made an honest woman of you."

Was it a proposal or a joke? For now, Megan decided to let the remark pass. "Forgive me for leaving," she murmured. "I was so upset, I jumped to conclusions. I shouldn't have gone without giving us a chance to talk."

"And I should never have let you go." His arms tightened around her. "But maybe this was meant to happen. Maybe this was what it took, for two stubborn souls like us to work things out and find each other. I'll confess it was the money at first. But then it wasn't. It was you. All you."

"So you never found out what Nick did with the money?"

"No, and I don't give a damn. It's in the past, over and done with."

His kiss was deep and heartfelt. Megan's response sent quivers to the tips of her toes.

She nestled closer, resting her head in the hollow of his shoulder. "About what you told me a minute ago, when you said it was time to make an honest woman of me…"

He drew her closer with a raw laugh. "More than that. I love you, Megan, and I want a life with you and our child— maybe even our children. I'm prepared to marry you the minute I can get you in front of a preacher."

"You mean that?" She gave him an impish look.

"Absolutely." His arms tightened around her.

"You're sure?"

"Hell, yes, I'm sure. Why?"

"Because there's something you might not know about Sam Watson. He's not just a doctor. He's also an ordained minister."

Epilogue

They were married the next day. The ceremony had been brief and simple, performed by Sam and witnessed by Saida, a few of the volunteers and the pilot of the plane. Even with no flowers, no music, no gown and no ring as yet, it had been everything Megan could have wished for—tender, romantic and meaningful.

They'd taken the supply plane back to Nairobi. From there they'd boarded Cal's jet for America, with a side trip to Arusha.

Harris had been so delighted by their news of the baby and the wedding that Megan had almost feared another attack. Surprisingly, the old man had followed his doctor's orders. He'd cut back on his drinking and his work, handling the business end of his company while Gideon replaced him as head guide. And he'd hinted, with a sly wink, that he was dating a sexy widow.

Ironically, on the way home, Cal had received an email

from Harlan Crandall. A Las Vegas casino owner had recognized a photo of Nick as the compulsive gambler who, under a different name, had lost millions at the gaming tables. Nick had also bet heavily on horse races and sports events, losing a good deal more than he won. Megan had been dismayed by the discovery of her late husband's secret life. But the fact that he'd gambled away the money was proof enough that Nick had been the sole embezzler, and that the money was truly gone.

In the two years that had passed since that time, Megan hadn't been back to Africa. With an active toddler son to look after and another baby on the way, she was busy with the family she'd wanted so much. But she'd left a piece of her heart with the refugees of Darfur. Here at home, she'd become an advocate for their cause, helping Cal set up a branch of the foundation to educate their young people.

Tonight she stood at the darkened window of her San Francisco home, watching the rain that streamed in a silver curtain off the overhanging roof. The sound of rain always brought back memories of her time in Africa. Tonight, because of the precious piece of paper in her hand, those memories were especially poignant.

"What's that you've got?" Cal had come up behind her. His hands slid around her waist to cradle the happy roundness of her belly. His lips brushed the nape of her neck.

"It's a letter," she said. "From Saida."

She didn't need to tell him what the letter meant. The last time they'd heard from the girl was a year ago, when she'd been struggling with the decision to leave Darfur and go to school in Nairobi. Her little band of warriors had been shrinking. Two of the girls, sadly, had died. Others had left for a different life—marriage, babies, work, a few for school. Passionate and loyal, Saida had been one of the last holdouts. But finally even she had abandoned the mountain camp to help her people another way, by getting an education.

"How's she doing?" Cal pulled his wife closer, rocking her gently against him.

"Wonderfully, it seems. She loves school, and she's getting excellent marks. She says she wants to become a doctor."

"She's a bright girl. She just might make it." Cal trailed a line of kisses down Megan's shoulder.

"I was thinking." Megan closed her eyes, savoring his closeness. "When she's ready for college, we could sponsor her and bring here, to San Francisco."

"Saida at Berkeley?" Cal chuckled. "Now there's a scary thought. I hope she's not still packing that AK-47."

"Stop it, you big tease! She'd do fine, and you know it!" Turning, Megan planted a playful kiss on his mouth.

Cal deepened the kiss with an intimate flick of his tongue. "Isn't it about our bedtime?" he murmured.

She snuggled against him. "You know, I was just thinking the same thing."

Laughing, he swept her into his arms and carried her off to bed, leaving Saida's letter alone with the rain.

* * * * *

If you liked A SINFUL SEDUCTION,
pick up these other emotional stories from
Elizabeth Lane

IN HIS BROTHER'S PLACE
THE SANTANA HEIR
THE NANNY'S SECRET

Available now from Harlequin Desire!

REQUEST YOUR FREE BOOKS!
2 FREE NOVELS PLUS 2 FREE GIFTS!

HARLEQUIN®

Desire

ALWAYS POWERFUL, PASSIONATE AND PROVOCATIVE

YES! Please send me 2 FREE Harlequin Desire® novels and my 2 FREE gifts (gifts are worth about $10). After receiving them, if I don't wish to receive any more books, I can return the shipping statement marked "cancel." If I don't cancel, I will receive 6 brand-new novels every month and be billed just $4.55 per book in the U.S. or $4.99 per book in Canada. That's a savings of at least 13% off the cover price! It's quite a bargain! Shipping and handling is just 50¢ per book in the U.S. and 75¢ per book in Canada.* I understand that accepting the 2 free books and gifts places me under no obligation to buy anything. I can always return a shipment and cancel at any time. Even if I never buy another book, the two free books and gifts are mine to keep forever.

225/326 HDN F4ZC

Name	(PLEASE PRINT)	
Address		Apt. #
City	State/Prov.	Zip/Postal Code

Signature (if under 18, a parent or guardian must sign)

Mail to the **Harlequin® Reader Service:**
IN U.S.A.: P.O. Box 1867, Buffalo, NY 14240-1867
IN CANADA: P.O. Box 609, Fort Erie, Ontario L2A 5X3

Want to try two free books from another line?
Call 1-800-873-8635 or visit www.ReaderService.com.

* Terms and prices subject to change without notice. Prices do not include applicable taxes. Sales tax applicable in N.Y. Canadian residents will be charged applicable taxes. Offer not valid in Quebec. This offer is limited to one order per household. Not valid for current subscribers to Harlequin Desire books. All orders subject to credit approval. Credit or debit balances in a customer's account(s) may be offset by any other outstanding balance owed by or to the customer. Please allow 4 to 6 weeks for delivery. Offer available while quantities last.

Your Privacy—The Harlequin® Reader Service is committed to protecting your privacy. Our Privacy Policy is available online at www.ReaderService.com or upon request from the Harlequin Reader Service.

We make a portion of our mailing list available to reputable third parties that offer products we believe may interest you. If you prefer that we not exchange your name with third parties, or if you wish to clarify or modify your communication preferences, please visit us at www.ReaderService.com/consumerschoice or write to us at Harlequin Reader Service Preference Service, P.O. Box 9062, Buffalo, NY 14269. Include your complete name and address.

"**W**ould you like to dance, Ms. Sinclair?"

She glanced at her uncomfortable-looking high heels.
"I...hadn't thought I would be dancing."

Laughing, Chance Lassiter bent down to whisper close
to her ear. "I'm from the school of stand in one place and
sway."

Her delightful laughter caused a warm feeling to spread
throughout his chest. "I think that's about all I'll be able to
do in these shoes anyway."

When she placed her soft hand in his and stood up to walk
out onto the dance floor with him, an electric current shot
straight up his arm. He wrapped his arms loosely around her
and smiled down at her upturned face.

"Chance, there's something I'd like to discuss with you,"
she said as they swayed back and forth.

"I'm all ears," he said, grinning.

"I'd like your help with my public relations campaign to
improve the Lassiters' image."

"Sure. I'll do whatever I can to help you out," he said,
drawing her a little closer. "What did you have in mind?"

"You're going to be the family spokesman for the PR campaign that I'm planning," she said, beaming.

Marveling at how beautiful she was, it took a moment for her words to register with him. He stopped swaying and stared down at her in disbelief. "You want me to do what?"

"I'm going to have you appear in all future advertising for Lassiter Media," she said, sounding extremely excited. "You'll be in the national television commercials, as well as…"

Chance silently ran through every cuss word he'd ever heard. He might be a Lassiter, but he wasn't as refined as the rest of the family. Instead of riding a desk in some corporate office, he was on the back of a horse every day herding cattle under the wide Wyoming sky. That was the way he liked it and the way he intended for things to stay. There was no way in hell he was going to be the family spokesman. And the sooner he could find a way to get that across to her, the better.

Don't miss
LURED BY THE RICH RANCHER
by Kathie DeNosky.

Available July 2014,
wherever Harlequin® Desire books are sold.

HARLEQUIN®

Desire

ALWAYS POWERFUL, PASSIONATE AND PROVOCATIVE.

THE SHEIKH'S SON
Billionaires and Babies
by Kristi Gold

Prince Adan Mehdi isn't normally one to back off from a beautiful woman, but when he finds out Piper McAdams is American and a virgin it seems like the honorable thing to do. Piper believes Adan's good intentions until his supermodel ex surprises him with their baby! Adan is abandoned by his family, so Piper agrees to show Adan the parenting ropes and play his pretend wife just until custody with his ex is settled. Things get steamy as the couple plays royal house. Could a real white wedding be in their future?

Look for THE SHEIKH'S SON in July 2014
from Harlequin Desire!

Wherever books and ebooks are sold.

Don't miss other scandalous titles from the
Billionaires and Babies miniseries,
available now wherever and ebooks are sold.

*Billionaires and Babies: Powerful men...wrapped around
their babies' little fingers.*

HER PREGNANCY SECRET

by Ann Major

The One Woman He Can Never Trust

Seducing Bree Oliver to keep the gorgeous blonde gold digger away from his too-trusting brother seemed like a perfect plan. Until a tragic accident changed everything. Now Michael North must honor a sacred promise. But watching over the pregnant widow is testing the tycoon to the limits of his control. He can't forget the night of passion that left him wanting Bree even more. Torn between desire and distrust, Michael's walking a treacherous tightrope, unaware of the shocking secret she's carrying....

Look for
HER PREGNANCY SECRET
by Ann Major in July 2014 from Harlequin® Desire!